"Do you still feel alone?"

He was surprised by how much he didn't feel alone at this moment, with her hand warm on his arm and her sharp green eyes gazing straight into his soul. "Not at the moment."

The air between them grew heavy and heated, as if a storm were brewing, thick with unleashed fury. The need to touch her overwhelmed him, until the only way he could quiet the thrumming in his ears was to lift his hands to cradle her face.

Her lips trembling apart, she lifted her other hand to his forearm, her fingers gripping tightly. "J.D.—"

He kissed her before his caution could kick in to stop him. He didn't want to be the careful man, the responsible man that life and circumstance had forced him to be. He wanted to feel something again. Fire. Hunger. Excitement. Even regret. Anything besides the numbing anger, grief and guilt that had driven him for twelve long years....

PAULA GRAVES

COOPER VENGEANCE

Harlequin®

TORONTO NEW YORK LONDON
AMSTERDAM PARIS SYDNEY HAMBURG
STOCKHOLM ATHENS TOKYO MILAN MADRID
PRAGUE WARSAW BUDAPEST AUCKLAND

For Amanda and Alicia,
two of my most loyal readers, and my good friends.

Recycling programs
for this product may
not exist in your area.

ISBN-13: 978-0-373-69552-2

COOPER VENGEANCE

Copyright © 2011 by Paula Graves

ABOUT THE AUTHOR

Alabama native Paula Graves wrote her first book, a mystery starring herself and her neighborhood friends, at the age of six. A voracious reader, Paula loves books that pair tantalizing mystery with compelling romance. When she's not reading or writing, she works as a creative director for a Birmingham advertising agency and spends time with her family and friends. She is a member of Southern Magic Romance Writers, Heart of Dixie Romance Writers and Romance Writers of America.

Paula invites readers to visit her website, www.paulagraves.com.

Books by Paula Graves

HARLEQUIN INTRIGUE

CAST OF CHARACTERS

Natalie Becker—When her sister Carrie is murdered, Natalie's sure her brother-in-law did it. But when a stranger insists the killer is really a serial murderer he's been tracking for years, will she trust her instincts—or his evidence?

J. D. Cooper—A widower still mourning his murdered wife twelve years after her death, he's come to Terrebonne in search of the man who killed her, the same man he believes killed Natalie's sister Carrie.

Hamilton Gray—Natalie's brother-in-law has an alibi for the night of his wife's murder. But Natalie's not so sure it's as airtight as the police think.

Mike Cooper—J.D.'s teenaged son is in Terrebonne visiting his grandparents. But once he learns his father's secretly in town, Mike will take any risk to find out what he's up to.

Doyle Massey—Natalie's colleague in the Sheriff's Department has always given her a hard time. Is there a hidden agenda behind his sudden friendliness?

Travis Rayburn—The young deputy is one of Natalie's only friends on the force. But is she foolish to trust anyone with her sister's murderer still at large?

Eladio Cordero—The South American drug lord has the Coopers in his crosshairs, thanks to a blood vendetta against J.D.'s brother Luke. Just how far does his reach extend—all the way to Terrebonne?

Chapter One

Natalie Becker crouched beside the new headstone, her eyes dry but burning. Seeing the name etched into the marble marker—Carrie Becker Gray—only amplified the anger burning a hole in Natalie's chest.

You shouldn't bear his name for eternity, she thought.

She stood up, finally, glad for the shade of the ancient oak, with its outstretched limbs creating a Spanish-moss-draped-canopy for her sister's grave. July and August would be hotter, but June was nothing to laugh at here in Terrebonne, Alabama. Unless you were right on the river or the bay, there weren't enough cool breezes blowing up from the Gulf to temper the sweltering heat and humidity. Even the shade offered only moderate relief from the heat and no relief at all from the mosquitoes and flies.

She batted at a large green bottle fly buzzing around her, ducking her head to one side to avoid the insect's dive at her face. As she did, she caught movement in her peripheral vision.

She whipped her gaze in that direction, the fly forgotten. In the pit of her gut, she was certain she'd see Hamilton Gray standing there, watching her.

She was wrong. It wasn't Hamilton. Not even close.

The dark-haired stranger standing a few yards away was a giant of a man, six foot four or taller, towering over even the larger of the granite markers surrounding him. He had broad shoulders, a massive chest, narrow hips and muscular legs. And his short, military-style haircut only amplified the aura of strength and authority.

Soldier? Maybe a cop, although being a sheriff's deputy herself, she knew most of the lawmen in this area and he definitely wasn't one of them.

Out on the access road, a horn honked, making her jump. She turned her head toward the sound, laughing a little at herself for being so tightly strung.

When she looked back at the stranger, he was gone.

She scanned the graveyard until she spotted him walking briskly toward the other side of the cemetery. His long legs had covered a surprising amount of ground in the few seconds her attention had drifted toward the sound of the horn.

Who was he?

Stop it, she admonished herself silently. *Stop seeing suspects everywhere you look. You know who killed your sister.*

The stranger was probably just an out-of-towner, here to visit the grave of a friend or relative. Out of curiosity, she crossed to the spot where he'd stood just a few moments earlier, growing more sure with each step that she'd find the explanation for his presence etched into the nearest marker.

But when she reached the marker, it was an unlikely source of enlightenment. The gravestone marked the final resting place of Mary Beth Geddie, who'd died a week after birth nearly a hundred years earlier. Not exactly what she'd expected to find.

She gazed toward the edge of the cemetery, where she spotted the large man walking through the front gates and straight toward a large black truck parked at the curb.

Illegally parked, she thought. She could ticket him and see who he was and what he was up to.

Her feet were moving before she finished the thought,

pounding over the sun-baked ground of the graveyard. But by the time she neared the gates, the black truck was out of sight.

She skidded to a stop and bent at the waist, breathing harder than she liked. She'd let her workouts go over the past two weeks while dealing with Carrie's death and the aftermath. Between the piles of food the good folks of Terrebonne had brought by before the funeral and the stress-eating opportunities that were part and parcel of dealing with her parents, Natalie had probably gained five pounds in the two weeks.

She had to get control of her life. Now.

She trudged back to her sister's grave, trying to feel something besides bitter anger and guilt. "I told you not to marry him," she said softly to the stone.

"I'm grateful she didn't listen," Hamilton Gray murmured, his voice equally soft.

Natalie whirled around to face her brother in law, who had stepped from behind the sheltering tree. Had he lain in wait for her? "What are you doing here?"

Hamilton's voice hardened in an instant. "Visiting *my wife's* grave." His eyes narrowed, giving his lean face a feral aspect. "The one *I* paid for, if you insist on becoming territorial."

You haven't paid yet, Natalie thought, seething at his tone. As if Carrie had been an object to cherish or discard at his whim.

"I know you think I had something to do with her murder, but I can assure you I did not. As can the authorities, as you well know." Hamilton's voice grew more conciliatory. "Natalie, I loved your sister. She loved me. I may not like to share my feelings with the world, but they exist nonetheless."

There it was. That convincing air of sincerity he threw on and off like an overcoat. It seemed to fool everyone she knew, including her father, who prided himself on judgment and his knack for reading people. But Darden Becker had one enormous blind spot—money. And if there was any family in South Alabama richer than the Beckers, it was the Grays.

"I don't expect you'll ever think of me as a friend, Natalie. You're hard to impress and even harder to know."

Natalie tried not to bristle at his words, not because he was wrong but because he was right. She wasn't easy to impress, and now that Carrie was dead, there probably wasn't a soul in the world who really knew her at all.

"I've accepted that you'll never consider me part of your family. But I'd like to give you brotherly advice, nonetheless. You should start listening to your therapist."

"My therapist?" She knew what he was talking about; the Ridley County Sheriff's Department had decreed that she see a therapist after her sister's murder. A nice lady, Diana Sprayberry, who spoke in a soft, calm voice that reminded Natalie of her first grade teacher. Dr. Sprayberry was a big fan of the stages-of-grief theory.

Natalie was not.

She wasn't in denial. She sure as hell wasn't bargaining. And if she was stuck on anger, there was a damned good reason. A sick son of a bitch had murdered her sister and, so far, had gotten away with it.

But how in the world had Hamilton learned about her private sessions with her therapist?

"It's not something that can stay secret in a town this small," he said, answering the unspoken question. "I know about your sessions. I hope they're helping."

She met Hamilton Gray's gentle gaze and hated him for the contempt in his voice, masquerading as pity. But she wasn't going to stand here like some sort of movie heroine and swear to God and anyone in earshot that she was going to bring him down for killing her sister no matter what it took.

He was right when he said the authorities would affirm his innocence. He had an alibi, of sorts—he'd made a call from his cell phone the night of Carrie's murder, and the cell tower signal showed he'd been three counties away. On business, or so he claimed. And since the sheriff's department had no other evidence suggesting Hamilton had killed his wife, or even had a motive to do so, they'd moved on to other suspects. Thanks to her father's business dealings, her family had plenty of enemies.

Natalie hadn't moved on, however. Even if they could prove to her satisfaction that Hamilton had been in Monroe County as he'd claimed, over an hour's drive from Terrebonne and outside the timeframe of Carrie's murder, it didn't mean he hadn't hired someone to kill his wife.

"I don't understand why you think I had a motive to kill your sister." Hamilton's plaintive comment tracked so closely to Natalie's thoughts that a chill skittered up her spine. He had a way of looking at her, his dark eyes so focused and piercing, that she sometimes wondered if he could read her mind.

Carrie had found his intensity exciting. Natalie had always found it disturbing.

"You know why," she answered in a voice strangled with barely contained fury.

"I was not having an affair."

"You were always gone—"

"On business."

"You didn't pay the same amount of attention to her as before," she added. "You were distant and brooding."

"And Carrie was spoiled and at times needy." His tone suggested he found those traits charming rather than annoying. "But honeymoons have to end sometime, Natalie. The family business requires much of my attention. I couldn't ignore it forever." His voice dropped a notch. "Maybe if you ever marry, you'll understand the situation better."

Her nostrils flared but she remained silent. After what he'd done to her sister, if he thought insulting her ability to maintain a relationship was going to make her lose her cool, he was right about one thing—he didn't know her at all.

Hamilton extended his hand toward her. "Can't we call a truce? At least for today, so we can both mourn your sister the way she deserves?"

She stared at his outstretched hand, loathing him so much she could barely contain the howl of rage burning like acid in her chest. "I'm done here," she said. "Carrie knows how I feel."

She walked away from him, forcing herself not to run, though every instinct she possessed was screaming at her to get away as fast as she could. She made it safely to her Lexus and slid behind the wheel, locking the doors. She leaned back against the sun-baked leather seat, shaking with a chaos of emotions.

"You're going to explode if you don't deal." Diana Sprayberry's gentle words drifted into her mental maelstrom. As if the therapist were physically there, methodically picking apart the tangle of Natalie's emotions and moving them to their proper places, Natalie felt the tension seep away, leaving her enervated. Only the blistering heat of the car's interior drove her to insert the key in the ignition and start it up so the air conditioner could dissipate the hellish swelter inside the Lexus.

She was off duty today, but the sheriff himself had called her at home early that morning and asked her to come in for a 2:00 p.m. meeting. Natalie knew Sheriff Tatum had asked Dr. Sprayberry to give him an evaluation of her mental state, but she'd been seeing the counselor for just under a week now. Surely that wasn't long enough to assess her state of mind.

As it turned out, apparently Dr. Sprayberry thought it was plenty long enough. The therapist herself was waiting in Sheriff Roy Tatum's office when Natalie arrived. Dressed in a steel blue variation of her usual prim business suit, Dr. Sprayberry was perched on one of the two armchairs in front of the sheriff's wide mahogany desk when Natalie entered.

She met Natalie's wary gaze with a mixture of regret and steely certainty.

"Administrative leave?" Natalie asked in disbelief when the sheriff got straight to the point. "You're taking me off the force completely? I don't even get desk duty?"

Tatum's expression revealed the same mixture of regret and certainty Natalie had seen in the counselor's eyes. "Dr. Sprayberry believes your inability to move past your anger at your sister's death poses a threat to the people of the county as well as your fellow deputies."

"And to yourself," Dr. Sprayberry added gently.

Natalie whipped her head around to look at the doctor. "So this is about taking away my weapon, not my badge. You think I'm either going to go on a shooting spree down at Gray Industries or I'm going to eat my gun?"

"Natalie," Tatum warned.

She looked at the sheriff. "I have another gun. I have a license to carry it. And as far as I know, we still have a Second Amendment in this country. You solve nothing by doing this."

The fire in Tatum's eyes told her she'd pushed the sheriff too far. "If you plan to ever step foot back in this department again, you will give me your weapon and your shield and keep the lip to yourself, Deputy."

She tamped down a retort and handed her duty weapon and her badge to the sheriff, slanting a look at Dr. Sprayberry. The therapist met her gaze, unflinching. Natalie headed for the door.

"And stay the hell away from Hamilton Gray," the sheriff added as a parting shot.

Natalie closed the door behind her and paused there for a moment, acutely aware of the curious gazes of her fellow deputies. She doubted any of them gave a damn whether or not she was suspended. Well, maybe Travis Rayburn, the rookie cop who seemed to have a little crush on her. And Lieutenant Barrow was always pretty nice to her.

But the attitudes of the rest of her fellow deputies matched those of her parents: what on God's green earth was Natalie Becker of the Bayside Oil Beckers doing working as a deputy sheriff?

She didn't care. She hadn't taken this job to make friends with her fellow deputies.

She kept her head high as she walked out, ignoring the stares following her out. She trudged to her Lexus and found, to her dismay, that she'd been in the sheriff's office just long enough for the brutal sun to heat the car's interior to a toasty 140 degrees. She lowered the windows to let out the hot, stale air and cranked the air conditioner up to high.

As she drove south, heading toward her house on the bay, the neon-studded facade of Millie's Pub visible in the distance drew her into a quick detour east. Millie's was a small place, little more than a hole in the wall, but the local law enforcement loved the place. For Natalie, the bar was more a curiosity than a home away from home, but she'd become accustomed to going there after work with the other deputies—her attempt, she supposed, to fit in with the others.

Why she was stopping here now, of all days—when she could call herself a deputy only on the technicality that Roy Tatum had suspended her, not fired her—she wasn't sure. God knew, it was too early in the day to drink.

But compelled by an emotion she couldn't define, she parked her car in a spot near the end of the building, stepped back into the fiery afternoon heat and went inside the bar.

J. D. COOPER SAW THE redhead from the cemetery enter the pub and stride straight to the bar, her long legs eating up real estate like a pissed-off thoroughbred. She bellied up to the bar and ordered a shot of Tennessee whiskey, downing it in one gulp. J.D. watched in fascination, wondering if she'd tell the bartender to hit her again, like a cowboy in one of those old Westerns his son, Mike, liked to watch on the classic movies channel.

She ruined the effect by taking a napkin from the metal holder and delicately blotting leftover drops of whiskey from her pink lips. She ordered a ginger ale chaser and settled onto a bar stool, drinking the soda from a straw and scanning the bar's murky interior with the eyes of a woman who knew she was completely out of place, which she was.

A woman like Natalie Becker didn't walk into a place like Millie's every day.

She was a deputy sheriff. Sister of the deceased. Daughter of one of the wealthiest men in the South. That much information had been easy to glean, even for a stranger in town.

Although technically, he wasn't a stranger. His connection to Brenda had opened a few mouths; all he'd had to do was mention his wife's name to some of Millie's customers to find out what he'd needed to know. Of course, he'd also had to suffer through the looks of pain and pity at the mention of her name. Brenda had been as well loved here, in her hometown of Terrebonne, as she'd been back home in Gossamer Ridge.

Stopping at Millie's had been a pure guess. At the cemetery, he'd seen the bulge of a weapon hidden beneath the lightweight jacket of the redhead's summer suit. Yes, this was Alabama, and a lot of women in the state carried concealed weapon licenses, but damned few of them wore lightweight summer suits in this unholy heat. That left law enforcement. Cops got used to wearing uniforms of one sort or another, regardless of the weather.

J.D. had considered going straight to the Ridley County Sheriff's Department and asking if they employed any redheads, but that was a little too direct for his purposes. So he'd done the next best thing—he'd found the only bar in town that looked like a place where cops would hang out.

"Another Sprite? Or would you like something stronger

now?" The ponytailed waitress stopped at J.D.'s table, her tone a little more friendly than it had been earlier, when he'd ordered a soda instead of liquor.

"I'm good," he said, earning a frown. The waitress drifted off toward more lucrative tables.

For a Wednesday mid-afternoon, the place was doing decent business. Some of the customers were farmers taking a beer break during the heat of the day, while others were workers coming off a seven-to-three shift at the chicken-processing plant a couple of miles away. No police had dropped by yet.

None but Natalie Becker.

Her wandering gaze finally drifted J.D.'s way. Her clear green eyes met his and she gave a start of surprise.

What would she do? he wondered, seeing a flicker of indecision in those pretty eyes. Pretend she hadn't seen him before? Come over and ask him his business?

Since he was trying to keep a low profile while he was here in Terrebonne, he should be hoping for the former. But Natalie Becker had information he needed—more information, probably, than anyone else on the police force—given her relationship to Carrie Gray. So he felt a thrill of satisfaction when she got up from her stool at the bar and walked slowly in his direction.

He stood as she came near, his sudden movement catching her off guard, halting her forward movement. Her watchful gaze made J.D. reconsider his earlier comparison to a thoroughbred. This Natalie Becker was a feral cat, all wary green eyes and sinewy-muscles bunched, ready for flight.

"Who are you?" Her low, cultured voice rose over the twang of a George Strait ballad on the corner jukebox.

"J. D. Cooper." He extended his hand politely.

She ignored his outstretched hand, moving forward slowly until she was even with his table. "You were at the cemetery."

"Yes."

"Why?"

"Visiting a grave."

"Mary Beth Geddie?"

He frowned, confused. "Who?"

"That's the name on the gravestone where you were standing."

"Oh."

"You weren't visiting her grave?"

"No. I was visiting your sister's."

Her eyes narrowed. "Who the hell are you?"

"J. D. Cooper."

She winced with frustration. "Is that supposed to mean something to me? What did you want? Why were you visiting my sister's grave?"

He cocked his head, wondering why she hadn't jumped to the obvious conclusion. "You aren't wondering if I'm the one who killed her?"

Her mouth dropped open, but she didn't speak for a moment as if he'd rendered her speechless. Finally, she asked in a strangled voice, "Did you kill my sister?"

"No," J.D. answered. "But I think I know who did."

Natalie closed her hand over the back of an empty chair nearby and pulled it around so she could sit down.

J.D. scooted his chair closer to her and sat as well. Reaching across, he placed his hand over hers where it lay on the table. "Are you okay?"

She jerked her hand from beneath his. "I'm fine."

He raised both hands to reassure her he meant no harm. "I could get you some water—"

"I said I'm fine." The words came out in a sharp snap. She flushed, looking embarrassed. He guessed Beckers didn't make scenes in bars. "Thank you," she added.

He saw her studying him closely, as if trying to take his measure. He wondered what she saw. At a distance, he knew he looked younger than his forty-four years, thanks to keeping up with his Navy fitness regime even after he retired. But up close, the years of grief and obsession showed around his eyes and mouth. Someone had once told him he had old eyes.

"What do you know about my sister's murder?" she asked. "How do you even know about it? Where are you from?"

He reached into his pocket. She tensed immediately, her hand automatically sliding down to her waist, as if she expected to find a weapon there. Her lips flattened with anger.

J. D. Cooper finished pulling out his wallet to give her his Cooper Cove Marina business card.

"You work as a boat mechanic?" she asked.

"My folks own a marina up in Gossamer Ridge," he said. "It's a little place in the northeastern part of the state. When I got out of the Navy, I went to work for them doing boat repair and maintenance."

She flashed a quick smile. He wondered why.

She laid the card in the middle of the table between them. "That doesn't explain how you know about Carrie's murder. Did it make the news up there or something?"

"You're from a rich, influential family. One of you gets murdered, it makes news everywhere in the state." He folded his wallet shut and put it back into his pocket. "The Gossamer Ridge paper didn't give many details about the murder. Neither did *The Birmingham News*. But I know some folks around here, so I did a little digging."

"Why?"

"Because I think the man who killed your sister is the same man who killed my wife."

Chapter Two

Natalie sat back in her chair, watching him through narrowed eyes. "Your wife?"

He nodded. "She was murdered twelve-and-a-half years ago. Late at night while working alone at a secluded office building. Nothing else around for at least a half mile."

The air in the bar seemed to grow chill. Natalie hugged her jacket more tightly around her. "Late at night—"

"Just like your sister."

She swallowed hard. "What do you want?"

"Do you know anyone named Alex?"

The question threw her. "Alex?"

"That's the name he uses. I don't think it's his real name, but it could be a nickname."

"You know his name but you don't know what he looks like?"

J. D. Cooper's only answer was to pick up the business card and pull a pen from his shirt pocket. He wrote something on the back of the card and shoved it back toward her. "I'm going to be hanging around town a few days. Here's where I'm staying. My cell number's on the front of the card. I figure you'll want to look into what I'm telling you, so I'll leave you to do that."

He unfolded his long legs until he towered over her like a giant tree, casting a shadow across the table. "I'm going to keep looking into your sister's murder, whatever you decide. I just think it'll be easier if we didn't butt heads about it."

He pulled out his wallet, laid a ten dollar bill on the table for the waitress and walked out of the bar.

It took a couple of seconds for Natalie's legs to cooperate enough to go after him. By the time she burst outside the bar, he was driving away in the same black truck she'd seen at the cemetery earlier in the day. She noted the make and model—a Ford F-250—but couldn't make out the license plate.

Torn between irritation and curiosity, she returned to the bar and retrieved his business card from the table.

J. D. Cooper, she read silently, her fingers tingling with the memory of his big, warm hand closing over hers.

She had a feeling he was going to be a boatload of trouble.

J.D. CALLED THE MARINA as soon as he reached the blessed coolness of his motel room. The place was cheap but clean, and the bed was big enough to look inviting to a man his size.

Waiting for someone to answer, he picked up the files he'd brought with him. It was twelve years' worth of notes, police files and newspaper clippings he'd compiled since Brenda's murder. Most of the pages were dog-eared and fading, while others were fresh photocopies of papers that had already started to fall apart.

He'd handled them all, at least once a day, for over a decade. An obsession, he supposed, but he couldn't stop now. He was closer than he'd ever been, thanks to his brother Gabe's recent trip to a college town three hours north of Terrebonne.

Ironic, that. Gabe being the one to blow the case wide open, since he was the one who blamed himself most for letting Brenda down the one night she really needed him.

His brother Luke answered the marina's office phone, catching J.D. by surprise. Luke ran a riding stable and wouldn't usually be there at this hour. "What are you doing there?" J.D. asked.

"I turned the stable over to Trevor and Kenny, and I'm meeting Abby here for dinner with the folks."

God, he sounded happy, even though he had plenty of reasons not to be. Eladio Cordero, the South American drug lord who'd put a price on Luke's life—and the life of anyone he loved—was still out there, biding his time. But at least Luke was home with his family now. The Coopers were pretty tough, always ready to guard each other's backs. And Luke had that beautiful wife and kid of his to come home to every night.

J.D. tried not to envy his brother—all his brothers, really, who'd now found the kind of happiness J.D. hadn't known in over twelve years. Even Gabe and Aaron had been bitten in the backside by the love bug. Aaron and Melissa were getting married in a couple of weeks, and Gabe had come home from his trip last month to Millbridge with a cute little college professor named Alicia Solano in tow. She still hadn't said she'd marry him, but anyone could see she was crazy about him, too. And Gabe could be a bloody damned nuisance when he wanted something. J.D.'s money was on him.

"Have you picked up Mike yet?" Luke asked.

"No, not yet." His thirteen-year-old son, Mike, had spent the last couple of weeks with his grandparents, right after his graduation from eighth grade. Brenda's parents had come up to Chickasaw County to see their only grandson's graduation and ended up taking Mike back with them to spend a few weeks.

J.D. had used Mike as an excuse to head south to Terrebonne, but Mike wasn't due to come back home until just before Aaron's wedding. J.D. hadn't wanted his family to know his real reason for coming here until he found out more about Carrie Gray's murder. They'd worry about him, and J.D. was tired of being the object of everyone's concern.

"How's Stevie?" he asked aloud to change the subject.

"He's great!" Luke answered. "Abby's been teaching him to speak Spanish, and he's starting to get better at it than I am."

J.D. laughed. "Well, tell him *hola* from his *Tio* J.D. I'm going to hang down here a little longer. Tell Dad he can get Jasper Noble to take care of any boat maintenance issues that come up while I'm gone. Jasper loves being useful since he retired—"

"How much longer?" Luke couldn't hide the surprise in his voice. Though Luke had been away from the family for ten years before his recent return to the fold, he'd apparently heard enough family gossip to know J.D. rarely visited Terrebonne anymore.

"A few days. No more than a week." He hoped.

"Okay. I'll tell everyone."

"Thanks. Hey, is Gabe anywhere around?"

"He's out unloading his boat. Just came in from a guiding job. You want me to have him call you?"

"Yeah, do that." J.D. might not want the rest of his family to worry about him, but he wanted Gabe to know what he was really up to. After all, Gabe had put his life on the line to solve Brenda's murder just a few weeks earlier, taking on a psychopath who'd been holding Alicia hostage.

A psychopath J.D. intended to visit in the Okaloosa County Jail up in Millbridge as soon as the visit could be arranged. Because Marlon Dyson wasn't just a crazy stalker. He'd been partners with the man J.D. believed had killed his wife.

Gabe called a few minutes later, and J.D. gave him a quick rundown on his reason for heading south to Terrebonne in the first place. "I wanted to get the local view of things, just to be sure," he told his younger brother.

"And what did you find out?"

"It's our guy. I'm almost positive."

Gabe was silent for a long moment. "Do you think he's picked up a new partner?"

"That's a question for your girl, I guess." Gabe's new girl-friend, Alicia, was close to getting her doctorate in criminal psychology, and she'd been the one who'd figured out there were two killers at work in the series of murders J.D. and his family had been trying to solve. Over the course of those years, the "alpha" killer, as Alicia termed him, had worked with at least two partners that they knew of—Victor Logan, who'd died in a mysterious house explosion a couple of months earlier, and Marlon Dyson. "And while you're at it, I want you to have her call up her friend in the Millbridge Police Department and get me in to see Dyson."

"J.D., are you sure that's a good idea?"

"I think it's a damned good idea," J.D. answered firmly, ignoring the wriggling sensation in his gut that belied the confidence in his voice. "Dyson helped that son of a bitch kill three women in the past year. Maybe more."

"Even the FBI can't get him to talk. What makes you think you can?"

"I'm motivated," J.D. answered flatly.

"Yeah, I'm a little worried about just how motivated you are," Gabe responded.

"Don't try to stop me. You're already on my bad side for keeping this information from me as long as you did." His little brother had a bad habit of trying to protect J.D. when it came to this murder investigation. Some sort of misplaced guilt for having screwed up and gotten to Brenda's place of work later than he'd agreed, J.D. knew. Gabe blamed himself, as if he could have stopped what happened to Brenda if he'd just been on time.

But he couldn't know that. Nobody could. The cold air that November night had slowed decomposition, making it hard to be sure when she'd died. Could have been a few minutes before Gabe arrived. Could have been as much as an hour. He could have been on time and still been too late.

On the other hand, if J.D. had left the Navy when she'd wanted him to, she probably wouldn't have been working at the trucking company in the first place—

"Maybe I should meet you in Millbridge," Gabe suggested. "I could go in with you to see him—"

J.D. snorted. "Like you could stop me if I went after him."

"I figure the guards would take care of that," Gabe shot back flatly. "I'd be there to pay the bail."

J.D. grinned at the phone. "I'll be fine, Gabe. I promise." His grin faded. "I'm this close to finding the son of a bitch who killed Brenda. I'm not going to screw it up by losing my head."

Gabe's answering silence was an unwanted reminder of just how close to the edge J.D. had gone over the past twelve years. Wild-goose chases, con artists trying to earn a buck off his grief, the emotional roller-coaster ride of chasing leads that never panned out—they'd all worked together to crush his fading hope and lead him to some very dark places over the past few years.

His family had worked overtime to keep him from falling apart. At times, they'd been all that kept him sane.

He broke the silence. "Will you see if Alicia can set it up? And call me back with when and where?"

"Of course," Gabe agreed. "J.D., Luke said you haven't even seen Mike yet. You left town two days ago. What's the holdup?"

J.D. looked down at the files in front of him. "I don't like him to see me this way."

"Obsessed?"

"Focused," J.D. corrected. "I'm looking at files I don't want him to see."

"You've been doing that for a lot of years now. Looking

at things you don't want him to see." Gabe's voice held no censure, only a bleak sadness that resonated in J.D.'s own heart.

J.D. knew he'd let his grief and rage steal too much time from his kids, not seeing until too late that he was throwing away moments, hours and experiences he could never get back. Thank God for his parents, who'd given his children the time, attention and unconditional love he'd been too broken to offer.

He was trying to repair the damage, one step at a time. But Cissy was nearly grown up now, heading into her junior year of college, and Mike would be entering high school this fall, taking giant steps toward an independent life of his own.

J.D. was running out of time to fix things with his kids.

"Alicia's down in Millbridge this week, tying up some loose ends," Gabe said when J.D. didn't answer. "I'll get her to talk to her friend Tony about arranging for you to visit Dyson."

"That's the cop ex-boyfriend?"

"Yeah," Gabe said wryly. "He's not happy about her leaving Millbridge to be with me, but he's a decent guy. He'll help you out if he can."

"Thanks, Gabe. I owe you."

"Not in a million years." Emotion tinted Gabe's voice, and J.D. knew he was thinking about how he'd let Brenda down. J.D. didn't bother trying to talk him out of his guilt. He'd told his brother that he didn't blame him. He'd said what needed saying. Now it was up to Gabe to work through his own guilt whatever way he needed to.

J.D. knew a lot about dealing with guilt.

He said goodbye to Gabe and hung up, his mind already fast-forwarding to what he'd say when he finally saw Marlon Dyson face-to-face. He'd wanted to visit Dyson in jail as soon as Gabe had told him the whole story behind the man's involvement with the alpha killer.

Dyson had slipped up once and called him Alex to Alicia's face before clamming up. J.D. wanted to see if he could use that small chink in the armor to get Dyson to open up some more. But to this point, the Millbridge Police had been stingy with Dyson, refusing to let J.D. visit the man in jail.

Dyson had been the alpha's partner, apparently tasked with hunting and culling victims for the man he called Alex to stalk and kill. He'd been caught last month, attempting to go rogue by stalking and killing his own choice of victim—Alicia, with whom Dyson had worked as lab instructors at Mill Valley University.

So far, he hadn't admitted to anything but the attempt on Alicia's life, although police and prosecutors were gathering circumstantial evidence to build a case against him for the three coed murders committed in Millbridge over the last six months.

But J.D. hadn't had a crack at him yet.

For now, however, it was dinnertime and he was starving. He'd seen a little hole-in-the-wall diner down the road that had looked like a good bet for some home cooking.

At the diner, he ordered a barbecue-pork sandwich and beer-battered onion rings from a woman he quickly learned was the diner's owner, Margo, a bottle-blonde in her late forties. She'd pegged J.D. as new to town immediately and, like a lot of Southerners when strangers came to their small towns, Margo was friendly but wary—until she heard J.D.'s slow, Southern drawl and realized he was Alabama born-and-bred. She quickly warmed to him, sitting with him at his solitary table while he ate and telling him everything she knew about everyone in the diner.

By the time he polished off a bowl of peach cobbler and vanilla ice cream, he felt as if he knew the business of everyone in town.

He turned the discussion to Carrie Gray's murder, certain Margo probably knew more about what was going on in

Terrebonne, Alabama, than even the cops knew. "I ran into her sister—Natalie, I think her name is."

Margo's eyes lit up at the mention of the name. "Oh, lord, that girl sure knows how to stir up a mess. When she decided not to go into the family business, you could hear old Darden Becker whoopin' and hollerin' all the way to Mobile."

"He didn't think she should be a deputy sheriff?"

"Good grief, no. The girl went to Yale, for pity's sake. Can you imagine sending your girl to a place like that for four years, only to see her up and join the sheriff's department after all that schooling? I'm surprised he didn't ask for his money back!" Margo laughed with delight. "Oh, Natalie's a fine enough deputy. She was promoted to investigator just this past spring. Don't reckon old Roy Tatum would've done so if she wasn't pulling her weight around there."

"Is she married?" J.D. asked, though he wasn't sure why. It didn't really matter, did it? He hadn't even thought to ask about her marital status earlier, when he'd been asking people in Millie's Pub about her.

But that was before you got an up-close look at those big green eyes, Cooper.

Margo's gaze fell to the wedding band on his left hand, then snapped up to look him in the eyes. "Why do you ask?" Her voice was suddenly wary.

He felt a flush warm his face, as if she'd caught him at something he wasn't supposed to be doing. He forced himself not to cover the ring with his other hand. He wasn't pumping Margo for information about Natalie Becker so he could ask her out on a date, after all. He had nothing to feel guilty about. "No reason, really. Just wondered if her daddy disapproved of her choice in men, too."

"Suppose it would depend on the man."

"What did they think of Carrie's husband?"

"That she was lucky to catch him. Hamilton Gray's slipped

the noose more than once since he was a boy, though God knows every girl in town's been after him at some point."

"Even Natalie?"

"No, not Natalie. She never has liked him much." Margo lowered her voice. "I hear she thinks he had something to do with her sister's murder."

"What do *you* think?" J.D. asked.

"I can't see the motive. He wouldn't get her money—old Darden Becker made sure there was an airtight prenup. And I don't reckon he'd have tired of a pretty little thing like Carrie so soon after the wedding. Besides, I heard he had an alibi."

Alibis could be deceiving. "Say, do you know anyone around town named Alex?"

Margo's forehead bunched with thought. "I think Ruby Stiller over on Beacon Road has a grandson named Alex. Why?"

He couldn't tell her the truth, so he improvised. "I ran into a guy at the gas station yesterday. Said his name was Alex. We got to talking about fishing and he said he could show me some good spots, but I forgot to get his phone number."

"That's definitely not Ruby's grandson—that kid's in kindergarten."

"Maybe I'm remembering the name wrong."

"Well, if it's fishing you're after, you should hunt down Rudy Lawler. He lives up the road a ways—just out past Annabelle's, in fact, maybe a mile or so."

"Annabelle's—that's the place where Carrie Gray was murdered?" he asked, even though he knew very well it was.

"That's right. Carrie bought the restaurant a few months ago and was trying to get it ready to reopen." Margo pointed right, toward the west. "It's about a half mile up the road."

J.D. gently pushed his plate away. "It's been a real pleasure meeting you, Margo. I'll be back, I'm sure."

Margo smiled brightly at him. "You just tell your friends about Margo's, okay?"

She walked him out, waiting in the door while he slid behind the steering wheel. J.D. waved goodbye, then pulled out on the highway. But he didn't head back to the motel.

He headed up the road to Annabelle's.

AT 6:00 P.M., THE SUN was only just reaching the horizon, still hot enough to make Natalie wish she'd left her jacket in the Lexus. But she'd stopped off at her house to get her spare weapon, and she didn't like walking around with her holster showing, not even at a place as secluded as Annabelle's.

The restaurant had once been a favorite among Terrebonne locals, one of the few nice restaurants in the sleepy little bayside town. Then Annabelle Saveau and her husband, Marcel, had moved back to New Orleans to take care of Marcel's aging parents after Hurricane Katrina, selling the property to a real estate speculator who'd thought the restaurant and surrounding acres of scenic woods would be an easy sell.

Years later, it was still for sale when Carrie decided she was tired of running the Human Resources Department at Bayside Oil and wanted a different career. Natalie's sister had bought the place a couple of months ago.

It had become the place of her death.

"Oh, Carrie, why were you so fearless?" she murmured, walking around the low-slung building until she could see the back door. Carrie's body had been found in the kitchen, laid out supine, as if she were merely asleep. Of course, the slashing stab wounds in her abdomen, and the blood pooling around her body gave the real story away.

The sound of tires crunching on the asphalt parking lot in front of the restaurant set Natalie's nerves humming. Unsheathing her Glock 19, she eased her way back to the front and flattened her body against the side of the building to avoid being seen as long as possible.

The engine cut off and she heard a car door open. She darted a quick look around the corner of the building.

There was no mistaking the tall, broad-shouldered, dark-haired man walking to the front of the building. J. D. Cooper stopped in front of the door and tested the lock. The handle rattled in his hand but didn't open.

Trespassing son of a—

Natalie eased away from the building, edging into the darkening woods behind her. She'd left her car down the road, not wanting to be seen snooping around what was, technically, still a crime scene, since she was on administrative leave.

But if she didn't get to look around, she'd be damned if J. D. Cooper got to, either.

When she reached her car, she pulled out her cell phone and dialed 911. "I'm calling from Sedge Road, near Annabelle's. I just saw a man trying to break into the restaurant."

Chapter Three

"Look, if you'll just call the Chickasaw County Sheriff's Department and ask for Aaron Cooper, he'll vouch for me." J.D. winced as the handcuffs around his wrists bit into his flesh, glad Gabe couldn't see him now. Although he might have need of the bail Gabe had mentioned any minute now.

"We tried. He wasn't in the office." Deputy Doyle Massey, one of the department's investigators, had taken custody of him once he reached the station. Massey was a broad-shouldered man in his mid-thirties, with sandy brown hair and eyes the color of tree moss. He looked impatient, making J.D. wonder just how much work an investigator got in a department this size.

"Then ask for Riley Patterson. Or call the Gossamer Ridge Police Department and ask for Kristen Cooper."

Massey glanced at J.D. "How many cops are you related to?"

"Do auxiliary deputies count, too?"

Massey grinned. "You must be the black sheep of the family."

"Funny."

"What were you doing snooping around there, anyway?" Massey unlocked the cuffs behind his back.

J.D. rubbed his sore wrists. "Am I under arrest?" Nobody had read him his rights, but clearly he wasn't free to go.

Massey led him to a small interview room. "Take a seat."

J.D. sat across from the deputy, wondering how much he should say about his real reason for being at Annabelle's. His own family was sympathetic to his quest for justice, but he'd found over the years that the local cops would prefer he just butt out.

"At the scene, you said you were just curious about the place because it had been a murder scene. How did you know that, you being a newcomer to town and all?"

Oh, what the hell. If he lied, he'd just look as though he was hiding things. "Twelve years ago, my wife was murdered in Gossamer Ridge, in a secluded area, late at night. She was raped and stabbed to death. The killer left no evidence behind."

The deputy's eyes gave a small flicker. "Go on."

"There've been similar murders. In Mississippi five or six years ago. Up in Millbridge, Alabama, in the last six months—"

"Are you talking about the murders that college kid committed? He was already in jail when Carrie Gray was killed."

This must be how Alicia felt, J.D. thought, trying to explain her theory about the serial killer pair to Gabe the first time. "There are two people involved. Marlon Dyson—the college student—was only one of the two killers. The other one is the guy who actually does the stabbings."

Massey frowned. "So the kid was just along for the ride?"

"The theory is, he procured the victims. Followed them, scouted out their schedules, getting to know them so that he and the alpha killer could get the drop on them more easily—"

"Alpha killer?"

"That's the theory. The alpha killer wields the knife. The beta does the legwork beforehand."

"Whose theory?"

Here we go, J.D. thought. "A criminal psychology doctoral student figured it out."

"A student?" Massey sounded skeptical.

J.D. pressed his lips together tightly, growing annoyed. "A doctoral student. An instructor, really. And she's a hell of a lot smarter than—"

"She?"

"Yes, she."

"Let me guess—new girlfriend? Got you a pretty little young thing who comes up with this fancy idea, so you thought you'd snoop around to impress her by handing her a new case to ponder?"

J.D. stared at Massey, repulsed. "The girl's barely six years older than my daughter."

"And you're listening to her theories?" Massey snapped back.

This interview clearly wasn't getting J.D. anywhere. Maybe he should play the apology card and see if he could get them to just let him go without any further trouble.

"Fine—you don't buy the serial killer pair theory. But do you at least get that I wasn't there to cause any trouble or do anything illegal?" he asked Deputy Massey.

"You were already doing something illegal—trespassing."

"How did you know?" J.D. asked.

"Know what?"

"That I was trespassing."

Massey's eyes narrowed. "A 911 call."

J.D. tried to hide his surprise. Who would have called 911? The place was in the middle of nowhere, on a road that had seen absolutely no traffic in the short time J.D. was there looking around, at least until the deputies rolled up, sirens blaring.

Unless—

"Don't suppose you know who called it in?"

Massey looked suspicious. "What does it matter? Was she wrong—?" He stopped, flushing as he realized he had just spilled more than he'd intended.

So a woman had called it in. A woman who'd apparently been sneaking around the restaurant herself, if she'd been in position to see J.D. looking around the property.

Now, who did he know who had a reason to be at the restaurant—and who'd probably be more than happy to call in a prowler report just to get J.D. out of her way?

"Doesn't matter," he told Massey aloud. "You're right, she saw what she saw."

"Why do you carry a gun?" Massey asked.

J.D. was surprised the deputy hadn't asked that question first. "I have a permit for concealed carry."

"I know. We looked it up. But why the CCW permit?"

"Last November, some drug enforcers came gunning for my brother. They were sent by a drug lord named Eladio Cordero—"

Massey spat out a profanity. "Luke Cooper's your brother?"

"Yeah," J.D. said with a nod. "I carry the SIG for my own protection."

"Way I heard it, your family took out most of the bad guys by yourselves before the law arrived." Massey's smile was grim but satisfied. "I'd have liked to have a piece of that."

"Am I free to go now?" J.D. asked. "You won't catch me trespassing again."

"Leaving town?"

"Not right away," J.D. answered honestly. "I have to wait until my kid's finished visiting his grandparents."

"They live in the area?" Massey asked.

"Yeah," J.D. answered, realizing he should have dropped

his in-laws' names from the beginning. "George and Lois Teague. Do you know them?"

Massey's eyes lit up. "Why sure, everybody around here knows Doc Teague. He's been treating most of the town since we were kids. You're Doc Teague's—" The deputy's voice faltered as he put the clues together. "You're Brenda's husband. The sailor."

"Yes."

The deputy's expression grew grim. "I went to school a few years behind Brenda, but I knew her. Nicest person you'd ever want to know."

J.D.'s heart contracted. "Yeah, she was."

"I guess I can't blame you for going to extremes to find the bastard who killed her," Massey said, his demeanor completely changed. "But I can't really have you out there interfering with an ongoing murder investigation, Mr. Cooper. You understand?"

J.D. nodded. "I understand." He hadn't really figured the local lawmen would buy into Alicia Solano's two-killer theory without a lot more evidence. He'd just wanted to make the deputy understand he wasn't a threat to law and order in Terrebonne.

"I'm going to let you go now, but you can't just be going around trespassing on private property, you hear? Let us handle it. I promise you, if there's any chance at all the perp we're looking for was behind Brenda's murder, I'll personally bring the son of a bitch down. All right?"

The tight sensation in J.D.'s chest spread to his gut. Everybody really had loved Brenda. She was one of those people who just made life better. She should have died in her nineties, after a long, full and happy life, not at the painfully young age of twenty-eight in the parking lot of an Alabama trucking company.

"All right," he said aloud.

Massey walked J.D. out to his truck, which another deputy

had brought to the station. He returned J.D.'s weapon and holster to him. "Take care, Mr. Cooper. No offense, but I'd rather not see you in here again."

Same here, J.D. thought as he climbed into the truck.

He'd just be a lot more careful next time.

His cell phone rang before he reached the motel. He thumbed it on and answered.

It was Gabe. "You're set to talk to Dyson tomorrow morning at ten. You'll have to set out early—it's a three-hour drive."

J.D.'s stomach dropped. He'd been pushing for a face-to-face with Dyson for a month, but now that the time was imminent, he wasn't sure he knew what to ask. "I'll be there," he told Gabe and hung up, his knuckles whitening on the steering wheel.

The Millbridge police had already checked Dyson's background, on Alicia's request. Dyson had been a teenager, living with his mother in North Carolina, at the time of Brenda's murder. He didn't have any long, unexplained absences in his history. The kid wasn't in on Brenda's murder.

But J.D. was pretty sure Dyson knew about all the murders. When he'd been stalking Alicia, he'd left her a note warning her she'd be victim number twenty-two. Fortunately, thanks to Alicia's level head and killer swing with a crowbar, Dyson hadn't been able to keep that promise.

Apparently it had been Carrie Gray's tragic misfortune to become the twenty-second victim instead.

Back at the motel, he decided not to overthink what he would say to Dyson the next day. Instead, he took his mind off the trip to Millbridge with a phone call to his daughter, Cissy, who was staying at his parents' place while he was down here in Terrebonne. She'd wanted to stay alone at the house; but with Eladio Cordero still gunning for Luke and anyone he loved, he didn't like the idea of his nineteen-year-old daughter staying alone, even though she was as good a shot as he was these days.

She answered on the second ring, a little out of breath. "Hi, Daddy. Are you and Mike on your way home?"

"Miss us?"

"Well, you, maybe. Not the brat." But her voice was affectionate, belying her words. "Actually, it's kind of fun hanging with Grandma and Daddy Mike. I've really missed them while I was at college." Cissy was a student at Mill Valley University in Millbridge, renting a place in the same apartment complex where Alicia Solano had lived when she was in Millbridge— which was rare these days, as Alicia was actively seeking a job closer to Gossamer Ridge in anticipation of earning her doctorate later this summer.

"You can always transfer to a college closer to home," J.D. reminded her, hoping she'd agree.

Of course, his independent-minded girl-child didn't. "No, I like it in Millbridge. I have friends there. Besides, it's a three-hour drive—I'll be home all the time."

"Like you were the last two years?"

"You're such a dad."

J.D. grinned. Although there was a guilty little niggle in the center of his chest more than happy to remind him he hadn't been much of a good dad after Brenda died: spending more time chasing elusive justice than comforting his children. "I'm going to be out of pocket awhile tomorrow, so I thought I'd check in tonight and let you know."

"Alicia got you set up to visit Marlon Dyson?"

He sighed. "Does she tell you everything?"

"Better than telling me nothing." She softened her sharp retort by adding, "You ready for it? You want me to drive down?"

He didn't know whether to be touched by the concern in her voice or insulted. He was a grown man—her father—and his daughter shouldn't feel he needed her to hold his hand. "I'm ready. You stay up there and keep an eye on old Rowdy."

His old mixed-hound was getting on up in years now. He'd still been a puppy when Brenda died, but these days, he was starting to slow down. He was really more Mike's dog than J.D.'s these days, although there'd been nights right after Brenda's murder when J.D. hadn't been sure he could get through the long, bleak hours without that pup by his side.

"Call me if you need me. I can be in Millbridge in three hours. Terrebonne in six."

"I'll call you if I need you," he promised. "Ciss?"

"Yeah?"

"You know I love you, don't you?"

Her voice cracked a little. "Of course I do."

"Good. 'Cause I do."

"I love you, too. Call me when you get done, okay?"

"Will do." He hung up the phone and laid his head back against the pillows of the motel bed, staring at the ceiling above, where waning daylight painted a crisscross of lengthening shadows over the sheetrock.

He'd spent half the afternoon, it seemed, assuring everyone he knew that he was fine, ready to visit Marlon Dyson and see if he could get information the police had, so far, been unable to obtain.

But he wasn't fine. He wasn't sure he was ready.

And he was lonely as hell.

MORNING CAME ENTIRELY too early for Natalie, in no small part because her sleep had consisted of one long nightmare, a relentless replay of the same harrowing image: she was Carrie, and she was trapped in the cluttered kitchen of Annabelle's, the back door blocked by a junk pile of old appliances stored there for eventual removal, and the front door blocked by a darkened silhouette wielding a sharp, deadly knife.

She ran and ran and never got anywhere, and still the dark

figure came toward her, in calm, unhurried paces. He knew she was trapped. He knew he could do what he wanted to her, and nobody would be close enough to hear her screams.

Waking for good at 5:30 a.m., she dragged herself from bed and showered, then contemplated what to do with the rest of her day, now that she didn't have a job to go to. Her mother had told her she should come by the house more often, but by now, the town grapevine would surely have made its way to her parents, and the last thing she wanted to do with her day was spend it listening to her father's litany of I-told-you-sos.

Roy Tatum had also told her to stay away from Hamilton Gray, which she didn't intend to do, but it would be smart to keep her distance for the next couple of days, at least.

That left J. D. Cooper.

She'd hung around Annabelle's long enough to see him taken into custody. She'd been surprised the deputies had gone that far on a simple trespass, but she supposed in a place as small as Terrebonne, a brutal murder could put law enforcement on edge.

She'd followed the squad car to the police station, parking far enough away to avoid detection but close enough to see Massey walk J. D. Cooper to his truck about an hour after he arrived at the sheriff's station, sparing her the need to intervene.

After all, Annabelle's was her property now. Carrie had left it to her in the will. All that was left was the paperwork. She had a say in who was trespassing and who wasn't.

She ended up at Margo's Diner for breakfast. Margo herself was behind the counter, entirely too energetic for such an early hour. She poured Natalie strong, black coffee without waiting for the order and set the cup on the counter in front of her. "There was a man here yesterday who seemed mighty interested in you."

Natalie glanced up from the steaming coffee. "Dark hair, blue eyes, about the size of a grizzly?"

Margo grinned. "So you've met him?"

She answered with a low growling noise. So, now J. D. Cooper was asking around town about her. "What did he want to know?"

"Not that much, really." Margo blushed under a layer of makeup, and Natalie got the feeling she'd done most of the talking. She did love to gossip. "He asked if you were married."

Natalie arched an eyebrow. "Is that so?"

"I wouldn't think much of it. He's married."

"Actually, he's a widower," Natalie corrected, though she wasn't sure why she bothered. Margo would probably latch on to that piece of information and turn it into a big deal. She didn't give Margo time to ask any more questions. "Did he ask anything about Carrie's murder?"

"You know, he did. He wanted to know if I thought Hamilton Gray could have killed her."

Interesting. So he was open to her theory of what happened to Carrie. "What did you tell him?"

Margo blushed again. "I know you think it's Hamilton, honey, but I just can't see why he'd do it. It's not like your sister would get any of his money if they just divorced. And he's not going to inherit anything from her because of that prenup."

Natalie should have guessed Margo knew about the prenuptial agreement. "You know everything that goes on in this town."

Margo grinned. "I suppose maybe I do." Another customer entered the diner and drew Margo's attention away, leaving Natalie to drink her coffee in silence.

So, J. D. Cooper wanted to know if she was married. Why hadn't he just asked her directly?

J.D. WASN'T SURPRISED to see his brother Gabe waiting in the Millbridge Police Department when he arrived. "I drove down last night and stayed at Alicia's," Gabe explained, shaking his brother's hand. "Dad's taking my fishing clients this morning."

"You didn't have to come," J.D. said, although he was glad Gabe was there. The drive from Terrebonne had seemed to fly by, not giving him nearly enough time to prepare himself to see Dyson.

"I came for my girl, not for you," Gabe said with a grin. "But while I'm here—"

J.D. squeezed his brother's shoulder. "Any word from the university about her dissertation?"

Gabe's grin widened. "The last revision passed and she has her oral defense in three weeks." Alicia's dissertation on the psychology of serial-killer pairs had included her personal notes on Marlon Dyson and Victor Logan. "Her advisor thinks she'll do a bang-up job on the defense. In a month, I'll be dating a doctor."

"Mom will be so proud," J.D. murmured.

A man about Gabe's age with wavy dark hair and brown eyes emerged from a door down the hall and walked toward them. He smiled at Gabe and extended his hand. "I thought you were back home at the lake."

"I thought I'd drive down to see Alicia." Gabe shook the man's hand. "Tony, this is my brother J.D. J.D., this is Tony Evans, Alicia's friend."

"I like to think I'm your friend, too, Cooper." Tony shook J.D.'s hand. "I've got Dyson cooling his heels in an interview room down the hall. I figured you wouldn't want to do this at the jail. I'll have to stay with you, and there'll be two guards there, too. Plus, he's cuffed to the table. You ready for this?"

J.D. nodded. "Let's do it."

His stomach knotting with tension, he followed Tony to the interview room.

Chapter Four

J.D. recognized Marlon Dyson's boyish face from the photograph that had run in the Millbridge paper the day after his arrest. Tony Evans had emailed Alicia a copy of the article the day it ran, and she'd shared it with J.D. for his case files.

But the last four weeks hadn't been kind to Dyson. His cheeks were leaner, and his eyes warier, as he watched J.D. and Tony enter the interview room. He'd been shot by accident while struggling with Alicia. Lost a lot of blood—probably explained his paleness as well.

"Mr. Dyson, this is J. D. Cooper." Tony sat in one of the two seats across the table from Dyson. J.D. took the other chair.

"The widower." Dyson smiled. "I've heard a lot about you."

"From Alex?" J.D. asked, disturbed by Dyson's hungry gaze. Dyson seemed to feed off the tension filling the interview room.

"Alex?" Dyson replied innocently.

"The man you worked with. The man who killed those coeds here in Millbridge. And the women in Mississippi and Louisiana."

"That was Victor Logan, wasn't it?" Dyson asked, still smiling. "That's what I heard. Good thing he died, huh? Saves taxpayers the cost of keeping him in jail the rest of his life."

"You rigged a gas explosion to save taxpayer money?"

Tony had asked the question, but Dyson's gaze never left J.D.'s face. "I have no idea what you're talking about."

"Who is Alex?" J.D. pressed.

"I don't know." Dyson's hard face softened until he looked like an overgrown, scared kid. "How would I? I just made a stupid mistake. I let my feelings for a coworker push me to do stupid, terrible things. That's all. I swear."

"Stupid things like killing a janitor who got in your way?"

"It was an accident!"

"You shot him in the head."

"The gun just went off," Marlon moaned, starting to rock back and forth. "I didn't mean for it to happen! I don't know much about guns—I should never have had it with me—"

J.D. stared at him in growing horror as he realized the sociopath was actually on the verge of tears. Tony made a low groaning sound beside him, but the sound barely registered over the buzz of rage filling J.D.'s ears. It could really happen, he realized as Marlon stared back at him, blinking back what looked to all the world like tears of fear.

Put this guy before a gullible jury, let him turn on the little boy lost act and he might get away with a minimal sentence for killing the janitor and trying to kill Alicia Solano in the bowels of the Mill Valley University's Behavioral Sciences building.

J.D. bit back a growl of frustration and pushed away from the table. "This guy's small potatoes. He probably doesn't even know Alex's real name anyway."

Dyson's smug gaze faltered for a second.

"The guy who killed those women doesn't make stupid mistakes. Alex wouldn't trust a half-wit like Marlon here with his name."

"You can't trick me into telling you his real name." Dyson's chin came up defiantly.

"So you do know it?" Tony asked.

Dyson clamped his mouth shut.

He didn't, J.D. realized. Dyson truly *didn't* know the killer's real name, for exactly the reason J.D. had said. A guy who'd gotten away with murder for over a decade wouldn't chance revealing his true identity to someone who could testify against him later.

J.D. was back to square one.

BESIDES A HANDFUL OF bed-and-breakfasts, the only place for travelers to stay in Terrebonne was the Bay View Inn, a twenty-unit motel that, despite its name, was at least a mile from the water. On a clear day, from a second-floor room, it was theoretically possible to see the bay from the motel, Natalie supposed; but from J. D. Cooper's ground-floor room all she could see was the parking lot.

It hadn't been hard to beat the lock on the motel room door, which probably explained why she had found almost nothing of value in J.D.'s room after nearly a half hour of searching. He'd be foolish to leave money or anything of worth in a place like this. Not out in the open, anyway.

She stopped in the middle of the room and looked around, trying to clear her mind of distractions. Such as the distinctive masculine scent that seemed to permeate every corner of the motel room, a blend of soap, aftershave and—she took another quick sniff—gun oil. So he was carrying a weapon? She hadn't found one anywhere in the room, so he probably had it on him. And if he'd been carrying a concealed weapon, the deputies who'd picked him up last night would have already checked his CCW permit. He'd clearly passed muster, or he'd still be cooling his heels in jail.

She forced her gaze around the room one more time. If she were going to hide something in a motel room, something she didn't want anyone else to find, where would she hide it?

Her eyes gravitated toward the bed. The bedcovers were neatly in place, the pillows symmetrically positioned.

Shipshape, even. What were the odds the giggling teens Bay View Inn employed as housekeeping staff could make a bed so neatly?

After checking out the window to make sure nobody was heading toward the room, Natalie pulled back the bedcovers. The pillows sat side by side, positioned perfectly across the bed. But there was something odd-looking about the pillow closest to her. She grabbed it and discovered it was heavier than a pillow should be.

She opened the case and looked inside. Below the fluffy foam-filled pillow lay a thick file folder full of papers.

She pulled out the folder and opened it. The papers inside were photocopies of police reports, crime-scene photos, witness testimony transcripts, autopsy reports, even newspaper clippings—a treasure trove of information about a series of murders dating back over a decade. The deeper she delved, the more her stomach tightened, nausea rising up her throat in cold waves.

There was no photo of her sister's crime scene in this folder, though the top-most sheet of paper was a photocopy of the article about the murder that had run in the *Terrebonne Banner* the day after. But Natalie didn't need a photo; she'd been the person who'd found Carrie's body. She remembered exactly how she had looked—lying on her back, as if she were merely sleeping, with her hands flat to the floor next to her. A series of knife wounds across her abdomen had spilled blood onto the pale yellow blouse she'd worn that day, turning it crimson.

Every woman's body in this file could have been Carrie's. The position was the same. The women were curvy brunettes like her sister, and, in the handful of photos where the victim's eyes were open, their eyes were brown like Carrie's.

No wonder J. D. Cooper thought Carrie's death was connected.

Forgetting all about covering her tracks, Natalie pulled out all of the photos in the file and laid them across the motel bed, beginning to tremble as she saw the sheer number of photos involved. Sixteen women, once alive, now dead at the hands of what clearly was a serial killer.

Or two killers, if J.D.'s theory was correct.

The rattle of the doorknob made her jump. Her first instinct was to scramble to return the photos to the folder, but she quickly realized she'd never put things back the way he'd left them. She left the photos where they were and pulled her Glock from the holster at her waist. If it was J.D., she'd explain herself and hope he understood the desperation that drove her. And if it was an intruder, she was armed.

It wasn't an intruder. It was J. D. Cooper, carrying a newspaper in one hand and a dark gray gun case in the other.

He jerked to a stop in the doorway, instantly focused on the Glock in her hand. His eyes widened a notch.

She put her weapon away. "Sorry."

J.D.'s gaze swept over the scene, taking in the haphazardly placed pillows, the turned back bedcover and the photos laid out across the bed. His eyes blazed with anger. "What the hell do you think you're doing in here?"

"Trying to find out if you're for real," she answered, keeping her voice steady, although inside, she was cringing with shame at being caught breaking and entering. What on earth had she been thinking?

"Do you have a warrant?"

She licked her lips. "No."

"Then get the hell out of my room."

She couldn't get out of the motel room without moving past him, and right now, he was filling the doorway completely, blocking her exit. But she couldn't just stand where she was, so she started forward, her knees trembling as the full impact of her foolish decision hit her.

It wasn't enough that she'd broken the law by picking the lock and tossing his room. She'd done so without any thought of what would happen if he caught her. What did she know about him, really? He'd told her some sob story about his dead wife, and he'd talked up Margo, the town gossip, but how much of what he'd told either of them was the truth?

He made no attempt to move out of her way. She faltered to a stop in front of him, drawing herself up to her full five feet nine inches, and he was still several inches taller than she was.

"You couldn't look me up on your computers at the station?"

She lifted her chin. "I'm on administrative leave."

"For breaking and entering?" he shot drily.

She supposed she deserved that. "Because apparently the department-ordered psychologist thinks I'm a danger to myself, my fellow deputies and the public."

"Are you?"

"No." Though she couldn't muster much conviction in the denial, considering he'd just caught her snooping in his motel room without permission.

His lips curved, as if he could read her mind. "Did you find what you were looking for?"

She glanced over at the photos on the bed. "Maybe more than I was looking for."

"Your sister looked like those women." He wasn't asking a question, just making an observation. Carrie's picture had been included in the *Banner* article. He must have seen the similarities between her and the victims in those photos. It was probably what had drawn him here in the first place.

"I found her body," she confessed in a reed-thin voice, wishing in vain that she could be stronger and more professional at this moment. "She was lying on the kitchen floor at Annabelle's. Stretched out straight. On her back, with her arms by her sides. Palms down. You'd have thought she was asleep."

"Except for the blood."

Her gaze snapped up to find him looking at her, his

expression soft with sympathy. "Except for the blood," she agreed. "Twelve puncture wounds. Deep. Tore up her insides."

"He twists the knife." J.D.'s words came out in a growl.

Her chest ached in response. "Yes."

J.D. finally moved out of the way, crossing to the bed. Setting the newspaper and gun case on the bedside table, he silently gathered the photographs and returned them to the folder. He put them back in correct order—the way she'd found them before she had spread the photos out on the bed— apparently, he knew the folder contents by heart. He tucked it against his chest, holding it with one arm as he might hold a child.

The door in front of her was open. There was no reason she shouldn't leave while she had the chance. But a question that had nagged at her since the day before wouldn't remain unasked. "How did you know to come here?"

His head snapped up, as if he had forgotten she was still there. "You mean to Terrebonne?"

She nodded. "What made you think Carrie's murder matched the others you've been looking into?"

"She looks like Brenda."

"Your wife?"

"Your sister looks more like her, in some ways, than any of the other victims." His faraway gaze focused on Natalie. "Not much like you, though."

"Carrie looked like my mother," Natalie explained. "I take after my father."

"Brenda was from here. She grew up right here in Terrebonne." He set the folder on the bedside table and sat on the unmade bed, one hand smoothing the wrinkles she'd left. "Her parents still live here—George and Lois Teague—"

"No wonder Carrie looks like your wife. She's a distant cousin. Her mother and mine, I think—we didn't really so- cialize much." Natalie felt strange just standing in the open doorway, so she closed the door behind her and crossed to the chair by the bed. She paused before sitting, silently requesting permission. She took his slight nod as an invitation and dropped into the chair, her wobbly knees grateful for the respite.

J.D. glanced toward the file folder he'd laid by the bed. "What did you think?"

"I think those murders definitely seem to be connected."

"And your sister's murder?"

"Body position was similar. She fits the profile. But—"

"But you already have a suspect—your brother-in-law."

She knew everyone in town thought she was crazy. Or jealous of her sister's marriage. Or both. But Hamilton Gray was not the grieving widower he portrayed. He didn't even try hard to pretend with Natalie, as if he enjoyed toying with her, making her seem a fool in front of her family and colleagues.

"Have you ever known, in your gut, that you were right? Even if everybody else in the world said otherwise?" she asked.

"That's exactly how I feel right now. I know in my gut that the same guy who murdered my wife also murdered your sister."

"Then I guess we'll just have to disagree. Because I know Hamilton killed Carrie. He may not have done it with his own hands, but he was involved." Natalie leveled her gaze with his, making sure he understood her meaning. "Nothing's going to stop me from proving it. Not the sheriff, not Hamilton—"

"Not me?" When she didn't answer immediately, he added, "You called the police on me yesterday, didn't you?"

"Yes." No point in pretending she hadn't.

"Because you thought I was doing something illegal? Or because you wanted me away from the crime scene?"

"You *were* doing something illegal—"

"And you broke into my motel room. Let's call it even."

She sighed. "It's going to be hard enough for me to keep investigating my sister's murder under the radar without having to deal with you dogging my every move. I don't need that. So if you're going to play follow the leader with me—"

"I didn't follow you to the restaurant last night."

"Nevertheless, there you were. In my way."

"What were you going to do there?" he asked.

"Look around. See if we missed something."

He leaned forward, the movement bringing his muscular torso that much closer to where she sat. She caught a stronger whiff of the masculine scent that had haunted her earlier while she was searching the room. "Maybe we should work together."

It was the last thing she'd expected him to say. "Together? On the investigation?"

"Yes."

"You're not a cop."

"At the moment, you're not really, either. And I know these murder cases better than anyone else."

"You're assuming they're connected. I don't assume anything of the sort."

"Doesn't matter. You'll investigate your way, I'll investigate mine. I'll watch your back. You watch mine."

She frowned at him, hating herself for finding the suggestion even the smallest bit tempting.

His voice deepened to a velvety growl. "We want the same thing, Natalie. You want to stop the man who killed your sister. I do, too. I don't think it matters that we don't agree who he is. Maybe that's a good thing. It'll keep us honest."

He was making sense. She didn't want him to make sense. She wanted him to go away and leave her to investigate in peace.

But he clearly didn't intend to go away. So why not agree to work with him? She could make him think they were partners while she investigated around him. At least she wouldn't have to conduct her investigation while checking over her shoulder all the time to see if he was there.

"You're right," she said aloud. "We do want the same thing. So let's do it. Let's work together on this case."

His eyes narrowed a fraction, as if he found her capitulation a little too easy. She schooled her features, determined to appear transparent.

"Okay," he said finally, leaning back again, taking away that spicy, tempting scent that had damn near mesmerized her for the last few minutes.

She resisted the urge to lean toward him for another whiff, extending her hand toward him instead. "Okay."

His fingers engulfed her, his grip firm but gentle. A tingling warmth in her palm caught her by surprise, making her feel like a teenager with her first crush, giddy and lightheaded.

It passed quickly and she released his hand, scooting her chair back to put more distance between them. "I should go—"

"What are you doing tonight?" J.D. asked.

She looked up at him, quelling a sudden nervous ripple in her belly. Was he going to ask her out to dinner or something? "I don't know—I mean—" She stuttered to a stop, her cheeks burning. *For God's sake, Becker, get a hold of yourself.* "I don't have any plans. Why?"

His face creased with a slow smile. "Because we have some investigating to do."

Chapter Five

"This is investigating?" Natalie's voice sharpened with impatience. Her half profile was taut with irritation.

J.D. saw all the symptoms. She was where he'd been years ago, raw with fresh grief and driven to action to take his mind off the pain and the senselessness of it all.

But action wasn't always the answer.

"Just wait."

"Your Zen master act is annoying. And cryptic. Why don't you just tell me why you wanted to come back here in the middle of the night?" She gazed at the darkened facade of Annabelle's. The rising moon shed pale light over the building's whitewashed clapboard siding, making it glow faintly in the dark. The dashboard clock read seven thirty-five, hardly the middle of the night.

"Your sister's time of death was clocked somewhere between 7:00 p.m. and midnight, when you found her body." He glanced at her. "What were you doing here at midnight?"

Her brow furrowed. "How do you know her time of death?" she countered suspiciously.

"My brother, the sheriff's deputy, requested the report." J.D. had called Aaron this morning after the meeting with Marlon Dyson ended fruitlessly. Aaron had called J.D. back with the details before he reached the motel.

He could see the moment his strategy dawned on her. "You're trying to re-create the situation, aren't you?"

He nodded. "Have you ever sat here since the murder to see what goes on out here this time of night?"

He saw dismay in her eyes, as if she realized the idea should have occurred to her without his help. "No. But I should have."

"You're a little distracted by your emotions."

She bristled. "And you're not?"

"Constantly," he replied. "I've just had twelve years of practice keeping them in check."

She settled back against the seat, looking ashamed for snapping at him. Silence wrapped around them like a cocoon until J.D. thought the tension would smother him. When he spoke, it sounded like a cannon going off, even though he kept his voice even and low. "Do you have someone to talk to—"

Before she could answer, a sharp crack of gunfire split the air outside the Lexus. J.D. flinched, dropping lower in the car for cover. On instinct, he reached out and dragged Natalie down with him.

When the sound didn't repeat, he chanced a quick look over the dashboard and spotted movement in the woods.

"It's a hunter." Natalie's breath warmed his cheek. When he turned to look at her, her face was inches from his.

His heart knocked wildly against his sternum. "You sure?"

"Pretty sure. That sounded like a rifle."

"Isn't it off season?"

"If it's who I think it is, he's hunting for wild pigs. No closed season, although I've warned Rudy that he can't hunt at night. But he doesn't like chasing the hogs during the heat of the day during the summer."

"Rudy?"

"Rudy Lawler. These woods butt up against his land."

"Then we need to find him."

"Why?"

J.D. reached for the car door handle. "Because if he's hunting here tonight, he might have been hunting here the night of Carrie's murder."

BEHIND NATALIE, J. D. Cooper moved in near silence, threading his way through the trees and underbrush with the skill of a professional tracker. She made a mental note to ask him where he learned the Deer Stalker act, but right now, she didn't want to make any more noise than she already was. She'd never been a Girl Scout; her parents hadn't seen the need for such pedestrian pursuits for their girls.

Piano lessons and charm school had been their lot. Carrie had taken to both with the enthusiasm of a born princess. Natalie had found the lessons tedious and unfulfilling.

"There." J.D.'s voice wasn't even a whisper. It was a mere breath on the back of her neck, stirring the tendrils of hair that straggled loose from her ponytail. She struggled to control the shiver that fluttered down her spine in response, focusing instead on the dark woods ahead. She spotted a flash of orange, barely visible in the gloom, a split second before the underbrush exploded with noise and movement.

J.D. dragged her with him a few feet to the right as an enormous black boar burst into sight, squealing and grunting as he churned past them. Rudy Lawler scrambled into sight behind the feral pig, raising his gun to take aim.

"Don't shoot!" Natalie and J.D. cried out in unison. Natalie waved her arms, trying to catch the hunter's attention.

Rudy pulled up short, jerking his rifle to one side. He stared at them for a moment before turning tail and taking off at a dead run.

Beside her, J.D. muttered a profanity and took chase.

Natalie struggled to keep up. "Rudy, we're not going to cite you! Stop running!"

Rudy kept going, his familiarity with the lay of the land giving him a definite advantage. But J. D. Cooper was faster than a man his size had any right to be. It took him less than a minute to catch up with Rudy and haul him halfway off his feet.

Natalie caught up, her breath burning in her lungs. "Damn it, Rudy. I said I wasn't going to cite you!"

"Let me down, you big gorilla!" Rudy struggled against J.D.'s firm grip.

"Put him down," Natalie said.

J.D. settled Rudy on his feet, keeping a grip on the man's jacket collar to keep him from running again.

"It ain't officially sunset yet," Rudy said defensively.

"I don't give a damn if you hunt until dawn," Natalie growled, flicking on her flashlight and shining it in his face. "We just need to talk to you."

"Were you hunting here the night of May 19?" J.D. asked.

Rudy peered at him. "Who are you?"

"J. D. Cooper. He's consulting with me on my sister's murder case." Natalie ignored J.D.'s quick glance her way. "Were you here the night Carrie was murdered?"

"Maybe," Rudy said carefully. "I like to go walkin'."

"Did you go anywhere near the restaurant?"

Rudy's eyes narrowed. "Am I a suspect or somethin'?"

Natalie glanced at J.D.

"No," J.D. said. "But we're hoping you might be a witness."

Rudy seemed to be gauging what he could say without getting into trouble. "Didn't see nobody, but I might've heard somebody."

"What did you hear?" J.D. asked.

"Voices. Men's voices. Two of 'em. One was kind of low, the other a little higher pitched."

Two voices. Natalie looked at J.D. He returned her gaze,

his eyes glittering with excitement. Was he right about who killed Carrie after all? "Did you recognize either of them?" she pressed, not certain what answer she wanted to hear. She'd been so certain Hamilton was behind her sister's murder, but how much of that certainty was based on her sheer dislike of the man?

Maybe she just needed to believe the worst of him.

"I couldn't make them out enough for that," Rudy replied. His posture relaxed a little as he seemed to realize she really wasn't going to give him a ticket for after-hours hunting. "I didn't want to get too close—your sister didn't like me much. Said my huntin' would scare off the customers."

"Are you sure it was two voices?" J.D. pressed.

"Yes, two voices." Rudy's gaze flicked back and forth between them. "This ain't about huntin' pigs at night, is it?"

"Why didn't you tell the police about this already?" J.D. asked, unable to hide a hint of irritation in his voice.

Rudy bristled defensively, "I didn't reckon it meant much of anything. Might not have had a thing to do with what happened to Miss Carrie, and I don't go botherin' the police about just anything, you know. They're busy folks."

"What you mean is, you didn't want them to know you were hunting at night when it's against the law."

Natalie caught J.D.'s arm, giving it a warning squeeze. "It's really more a guideline than a law," she said lightly. She looked at Rudy. "Rudy, here's what I want you to do, okay? Promise me you'll do this."

Rudy scowled. "I ain't promisin' anything until I hear what you want me to do."

"Go to the police in the morning. Deputy Doyle Massey is the investigator on my sister's murder case. Tell Deputy Massey that you remembered something from the night of the murder. I don't care what reason you give for being out here—tell him you were walking your dogs or something. But tell him what you heard."

"Why can't you tell him?"

"Because I'm not supposed to be anywhere around the case."

"'Cause it was your sister?"

"Something like that."

"I don't think what I heard's gonna help the case any."

"Maybe it won't," Natalie conceded. "But it's context, and that's important to an investigation."

Rudy released a little huff of breath. "All right. I'll do it for you, Miss Natalie, 'cause you've always been real nice to me, and that ain't true of all the folks around here."

"Thank you." She realized she was still holding J.D.'s arm, so tightly that her fingers were beginning to tingle. She let go and shot a quick look at him. He stared back at her, an odd expression on his face.

Rudy grimaced. "Now the sun's gone down. God knows what that boar's gonna do to some poor farmer's crop tonight runnin' loose until daylight." He shot J.D. a pointed look. "I wouldn't think of breakin' the law. No matter how stupid it is." Rudy walked away, grumbling under his breath.

"Don't forget—Deputy Massey!" Natalie called after him.

"Will he call?" J.D. asked as they walked back to the car.

"I hope so." She unlocked her car door with the remote on her keychain. "I'll drop you off at your motel—"

"You hungry?" he asked.

She hadn't even thought about food since her breakfast at Margo's diner. She was starving, but she answered, "A little."

"There's a place down the road that serves great burgers—"

"Margo's," she guessed. "And if we go there together, by tomorrow, everyone in town will either know we've been to Annabelle's or think we're having an affair."

"Right." J.D. settled into the seat.

"There's a seafood shop near my house on Terrebonne Bay.

Amazing shrimp. We could buy a pound, fire up my grill—"
By the time her brain caught up with her reckless tongue, J.D.
was agreeing to the idea.

Had she lost her mind?

"You look like you just swallowed a fly," J.D. said.

She laughed nervously.

"Probably not smart to ask a stranger home," he added. "If
you're rethinking the invitation, it won't hurt my feelings."

Somehow, his words did more to reassure her about his
intentions than any background check would have done. "No.
I believe you're who you say you are."

"That doesn't mean you have to have me over for dinner."

"You need to eat. I need to eat." Keeping her voice light,
she shrugged, though a part of her still wanted to back out of
the offer. But not because she was afraid he was a homicidal
maniac.

She was beginning to find him an entirely different sort
of danger. Being around him made her lose all good sense,
and she ended up doing things like breaking into motel rooms
and asking strange men to her house for dinner.

What else might J. D. Cooper induce her to do before the
night was through?

TERREBONNE BAY WAS AN inlet off much larger Mobile Bay,
fed by the Terrebonne River. Waterfront homes lined up, side
by side, for several miles before oak trees draped with wispy
Spanish moss took over and the houses became fewer and
farther between.

They became larger and nicer as well, J.D. noted as Natalie's Lexus wound along the narrow two-lane road, the headlights giving occasional glimpses of the waterfront homes
along this stretch of the bay. She finally slowed as they neared
a gated driveway leading down toward the water, guiding the
nose of the sedan between the river-stone pillars at the opening of the drive.

He'd known she came from a prosperous family, but the sprawling clapboard cottage at the edge of the bay was a serious money kind of place. There was nothing ostentatious about it; though the house was large, it gave the appearance of modesty and casual charm. But J.D. had seen enough high-end lake homes to know what pricey real estate looked like.

"My uncle used to live here," Natalie said as she parked under the house between the stilt-like piles that held the main house several feet off the ground. "My mother's brother. He died a few years ago and left it to me. Dad wanted me to sell it and buy a place in Mobile. That was back when he thought I was going to work for the company."

"You dad is an oilman, right?"

"Bayside Oil," she said with a nod. "Don't get me wrong. I'm not one of those people who think oil is evil or anything. But the business just wasn't for me."

"Why the sheriff's department?"

"Why the Navy?"

He smiled, though he felt a bittersweet tinge of regret as well. "I wanted to serve my country."

"And I wanted to serve the people of this town." She unlocked the trunk of her car, where they'd stashed a cooler full of seafood. He carried the cooler, following her lead up the stairs to the cottage's front door. Inside, the cottage was simply appointed, the furniture spare but good quality. A long brown-leather sofa and several comfortable-looking chairs framed a low pine coffee table in the living area, where one wall consisted entirely of floor-to-ceiling windows that J.D. guessed would offer an amazing view of Terrebonne Bay during daylight hours.

"Those French doors lead to the deck. The grill's out there." Natalie took the cooler from him. "I'll get things prepared while you get the grill fired up. Everything you need is in the storage cabinet outside. And be sure to light the citronella candles or the mosquitoes will eat you alive."

J.D. headed through the French doors and found himself on a large redwood deck that wrapped around the entire back of the house. It was twice the size of the deck on his parents' lake house, and he'd always considered that deck to be enormous. At one end, a built-in grill island spanned almost seven feet of the deck. The storage cabinet Natalie had referred to was not the typical resin box he'd been expecting but a stainless-steel cabinet built into the grill island.

J.D. had to tamp down a giddy grin. Bloody grill heaven, and he got to wield the tongs.

By the time the door to the deck opened behind him, the citronella candles perched on the deck railing were giving off a flickering golden glow, the grill was fired up and ready to go and J.D. was playing around with the grill island settings to see what they did.

"Nice toy, huh?" Natalie's amused drawl drew his gaze away from the grill. She'd changed clothes, losing the lightweight business suit for something soft and filmy. The blue halter-cut blouse showed off creamy shoulders and a tantalizing hint of firm, round breasts where the V-neck dipped in the front. She'd let her hair down from its usual neat ponytail to fall in cinnamon waves around her face, softening its sharper angles.

He forgot all about the grill.

She was wheeling a small serving cart behind her, filled with trays of shrimp and raw vegetables. "This look like enough?"

He nodded, turning back to the grill. A breeze blew in off the bay, stirring his hair and cooling his heated cheeks. *Don't think of her as a woman. It complicates everything.*

"Have I said something wrong?"

He turned, finding her looking soft and pretty, lit by the moonlight and the candles circling the deck. He wanted to kiss away the little frown line between her eyes and tell her everything was perfect. But the fact that he wanted to do either of those things scared the hell out of him.

"If you don't want to be here—"

He touched her before his brain could kick in and stop him. It was nothing out of bounds, a light brush of his fingers against the curve of her shoulder, but the air between them instantly crackled with energy. "I want to be here," he answered, his voice coming out in a hoarse growl.

"Too much?" she whispered, her green eyes gentle.

He dropped his hand away, guilt gripping him in a bitter vise. "I guess I wasn't ready for this." He turned away again, focusing on the lights sparkling across the waters of the bay.

"You've been faithful to your wife all these years?"

"Not physically, no." He met her gaze. "But I loved her. I still do."

Her frown deepened. "I'm sure you always will. But that doesn't mean you can't move forward."

His lips curved, but he wasn't feeling much humor. "I know that. Academically, anyway. My mother's constantly worrying about me. She keeps saying Brenda wouldn't want me to build a shrine to her. She'd want me to be happy again. And it's true. Brenda would be horrified to see me now."

"But you can't stop."

He released a harsh sigh. "Not until the bastard who killed her—who killed all those women—is dead or locked away where he can't ever kill again. Then maybe I can have a life again."

"So, let's find him."

He made himself look at her again. The softness he'd seen in her before was gone, replaced by a steely gaze and a jaw so squared and determined that he was half convinced it had been chiseled from granite. "You have your own murder to solve. Or are you agreeing they're one and the same?"

"I'm saying it's an angle worth pursuing." The curl of her

lips carved a dimple in one of her lean cheeks. "Get the shrimp on. I'll be right back." She disappeared into the house.

When she came back out a few minutes later, she'd changed clothes again, wearing a faded, oversized University of Alabama T-shirt and a pair of baggy sweat pants. Her hair was tucked under a BayBears cap, and her face was makeup free.

He still wanted to kiss her. But he appreciated her effort.

Dinner turned out to be more comfortable than he'd expected. The good food and the gorgeous bay view went a long way toward lightening his mood, and Natalie turned out to be a charming dinner companion. Dinner and their relaxed conversation seemed to chisel down the harder edges of her personality, exposing a bright woman full of quirky humor and insightful observations.

His cell phone rang around ten, a shocking intrusion on the calm scene. He checked the screen and saw his brother Gabe's number. "I have to get this."

Natalie picked up their plates and took them into the kitchen, giving him privacy.

"Hey, Gabe, what's up?"

Without preamble, Gabe said, "Marlon Dyson is dead."

Chapter Six

"You don't buy the suicide angle." Natalie broke the tense silence that had fallen between them since they began the drive back to J.D.'s motel room. The call from his brother had ended any thoughts of a longer evening together, which was probably for the best, since neither of them needed any more complications in their lives at the moment.

But as they neared the Bay View Inn, Natalie wished for a moment that they were back on her deck, sipping coffee and relaxing, with nothing more pressing to think about than how soon the citronella candles would flicker out and leave them at the mercy of the mosquitoes.

"I don't know," J.D. answered. "He knew we didn't have anything on him except the attempted murder of Alicia. He had no priors, he was young and educated—he had to know he had a good chance at a light sentence. No way he drinks poison on purpose."

"It sounds suspicious," she conceded. "But you really think the alpha killer arranged his murder in jail? How could he have that sort of reach?"

"I don't know," he admitted. "I just know he likes to tie up his loose ends. I think that's why he had Dyson kill Victor last month. At least, I'm pretty sure Dyson did it."

"If you're right, the alpha killer let Logan live for how long—four years?"

J.D. nodded.

"Why kill him after four years? Clearly, he hadn't spilled any information about the alpha in that time."

"Last month, Victor spotted my brother Jake's wife, Mariah, on a television newscast after a bad tornado hit Buckley, Mississippi. He knew Mariah from before—he'd been sort of her mentor. Gave her a place to stay, turned her into his own private student—Logan saw himself as an intellectual. Self-taught, but Mariah says he really did have an insatiable thirst for learning. Anyway, he went after her and Jake. I guess it made him seem too dangerous to keep around."

The lights of the motel gleamed down the road ahead, and Natalie felt a twinge of regret that the evening was about to be officially over. She parked next to his truck in front of the room and walked him to the door, noticing that the neon glow of the motel's marquee at the front didn't seem to carry all the way here to the far end of the motel. This end of the structure seemed to wallow in darkness, giving the old building an almost sinister appearance. Natalie was relieved when J.D. unlocked the door to his room and reached inside to flick on the light.

He stuck his head inside, took a quick scan of the place, then turned to look at her. "Thanks for dinner. I think I'm in love with your grill."

She laughed. "I could tell your intentions toward it weren't entirely honorable."

"I wish—" He stopped, as if he had reconsidered his words, and she figured he'd just stop there. But he squared his shoulders and looked her dead in the eye, his gaze so intense she felt it as surely as if he'd touched her. "I wish Brenda hadn't been murdered. If she had to die, I wish it had been something else. Something quick and painless for her. Something we could grieve and move on from."

In her chest, her heart gave a little squeeze. "But you can't. I do understand."

"Maybe you do." He cupped her cheek for a moment in his big, work-roughened hand. The touch was light and undemanding, but she seemed to feel it all the way to her marrow.

He dropped his hand away, leaving her feeling oddly bereft. "I meant my offer earlier. We should work your sister's case together. We did pretty well tonight, didn't we?"

"Yeah, we did." She wondered if Rudy Lawler was really going to call Doyle Massey to tell him about hearing the voices outside the restaurant the night Carrie died. Roy Tatum had picked a terrible time to put her on administrative leave. She couldn't even call Massey to check up on Rudy without risking a bad reaction from the sheriff. "I should go."

He took a step back. "Be careful."

She nodded. "I have a Glock in the car."

His lips curved. "You're just trying to get me hot and bothered now, aren't you?"

She laughed. "Well, that, and I really do have a Glock in the car." She lifted her hand in farewell and headed across the lot to her car. She took a quick glance behind her and saw that J.D. had already closed the door and gone inside.

She sighed, pulling her keys from the pocket of her jeans as she neared the Lexus, stopping as she heard the sound of a car approaching. Turning her head to spot the vehicle, she froze as she saw a dark sedan bearing down on her, its lights extinguished. But even in the low light of the parking lot, she couldn't miss the glint of moonlight on the barrel of a pistol.

She propelled herself backward, with no idea what lay behind her, and scrambled for cover behind the nearest vehicle, a low-slung black sedan. She heard four thuds shake the car, though the expected cracks of gunfire didn't come, only flat, blatting noises. Sound suppressor, she thought, her mind whirling madly.

She heard the car slow into the turn at the end of the parking lot, its brakes shrieking.

Natalie scrambled backward crab-style, her palms scraping on the asphalt. She heard a door open behind her, and a couple of seconds later, strong arms wrapped around her, pulling her to her feet. She looked up to find J.D. gazing down at her, his eyes wide with alarm as they looked her over for signs of injury.

"What the hell just happened?" he asked.

She spotted other guests peeking out the doors of their motel rooms, drawn by the noise of the squealing brakes. She lowered her voice so that only J.D. could hear her. "Someone tried to shoot me," she breathed.

His gaze snapped up toward the end of the parking lot, where the darkened sedan had already disappeared down the highway. "Here in the parking lot?" He kept his voice equally low. "I didn't hear any shots."

"Sound suppressor," she replied. "I couldn't get a good look—they drove with no headlights."

He uttered a quick, guttural epithet. "I didn't get a look at the car. Did you?"

"I was more focused on the gun bearing down on me." She shook her head. "I think it was a Mercury. No idea of the model. Might have been black, might have been dark blue or dark green—hard to tell." She peered up at the street lamp that should have illuminated this part of the parking lot. The light was out, which explained the darkness in this section of the motel lot.

"Was that light out last night?" she asked.

He followed her gaze. "Yeah. I noticed it last night."

"Okay."

"You think maybe someone put it out on purpose?" He put his arm around her and led her into his room, closing the door.

She wasn't sure *what* she thought. Her heart still stuttered like a snare drum, and her head ached from the tense set of her muscles. "All I know is that it wasn't random. The shooter didn't fire until the car got right up on me."

He settled her on the side of the bed and sat next to her, his hand warm between her shoulders. "We need to report this."

She winced at the thought of her colleagues coming out on this call. But she couldn't just ignore an attempt on her life.

J.D. made the call while she examined her injuries. The heels of her hands had taken the brunt of the damage, raw, red scrapes marring the skin from her thumb to the outside edge of her hand. In the bathroom, she washed the asphalt grit and grime out of the scrapes, wincing as the soapy water stung like fire.

"Ouch," J.D. murmured from the doorway, making her jump.

She smiled sheepishly. "Don't suppose you have a first-aid kit lying around?"

"Matter of fact, I do." He handed her a clean towel to dry her hands and went back into the bedroom area. He dug in his suitcase until he emerged with a soft-sided first-aid bag. With a quick unzip, he spread the array of ointments, bandages and medicines on the bed. "Sit and I'll do it for you."

He held out his hand, palm up, and she gingerly laid the back of her hand in his, no longer surprised by the slight tingle in her flesh where their skin touched. She cleared her throat and tried to ignore the thrumming sensation building in her arms and legs. "What did you tell the dispatcher when you called 911?"

"I told her nobody was hurt, but there had been a drive-by shooting and we needed to report it and give a statement. She said she'd have an investigator out here as soon as she could."

"Are we sure nobody else is hurt?" She winced again as he wiped an antiseptic pad over her scrapes.

"Sorry," he murmured. "I saw the people on either side of me looking outside to see what the noise was about. I didn't see anyone who looked hurt. How many shots were there?

"I heard four hit that black car parked next to your truck. I don't know if any hit the truck." She shot him an apologetic look. "Might've."

"We'll check it out when the deputies get here."

She couldn't hold back a frown.

"Any particular reason you don't want the deputies to come?"

She shook her head. "I'm just not a favorite of anybody I work with." She chuckled grimly. "Some of them probably sympathize with the shooters."

"Are you hard to work with?" He didn't sound as if he'd be surprised to hear she was difficult.

She tried not to bristle. "I don't think I am."

His gaze angled up to meet hers briefly, a hint of skepticism glittering in his eyes.

"You think I'm difficult?"

"I think you're complicated. And a little defensive." He finished putting the last bandage on her hand. "All done."

"Defensive?"

He gave her another silent look.

He was right. She was defensive. And prickly. And at the moment, simmering with a slow roil of anger—at herself, at Hamilton Gray, at her parents and her coworkers and the whole damn world that kept on spinning, day in and day out, as if her sister wasn't lying six feet under the earth in a grave marked with her killer's last name.

Or was she wrong about that, too? Did Carrie's murder have nothing at all to do with her husband and the difficulties she'd been experiencing in their marriage?

She folded her hands in her lap and looked up at J.D., who was putting the leftover supplies back into the first aid kit. "What if we're both wrong?"

He stopped in the middle of zipping the bag and met her gaze. "Wrong about what?"

"About Carrie's death. What if it wasn't Hamilton or your alpha and beta serial-killer pair?" She pushed to her feet, the new theory racing through her mind making her feel edgy and full of restless energy. She paced across the room to the window, pulling aside the curtains to look out at the darkened parking lot. "What if her death had something to do with being a Becker?"

"You think someone could be targeting your family?"

She moved away from the window, putting the solid wall rather than breakable glass between her and the outside world as she turned around to look at him. "My father is a wealthy oilman who can be ruthless in business. He's ruined people—not intentionally as far as I know, but the result is the same. He's fired employees, cut loose contractors—"

"Made enemies," he finished for her.

She nodded. "What if Carrie's murder was an act of revenge?"

J.D.'s eyes narrowed. "I don't know. The crime scenes were similar, weren't they? You've seen the photos in my files."

"Yes, but—" She pressed her lips together, frustrated. It seemed as if every time she took a step forward in her investigation, she only discovered more questions. "I don't know," she finally admitted. "I don't know what's behind it, but I think we shouldn't discount revenge or some sort of vendetta as a motive. People with grudges can be ruthless and dangerous."

"Tell me about it," he said drily.

"I don't think your determination to find the man who murdered your wife is the same thing I'm talking about."

He shook his head. "Actually, I was thinking about my brother Luke. He's got a price on his head—the whole family does, in a way. He was a Marine investigating allegations that peacekeeping troops in Sanselmo were selling American surplus arms to the rebels during the *El Cambio* uprising a few years ago—"

She nodded. Her father's company had holdings in the South American nation of Sanselmo, and during the six-month uprising, the violent rebel group *El Cambio* had targeted foreign companies to put pressure on outsiders to isolate the government in power. Her father had made a few enemies in the *El Cambio* himself.

"My brother was in one of those situations where you have to kill or you and a lot of civilians could end up dead, too. Luke shot a terrorist. Turned out he was the son of Eladio Cordero."

"My God." Eladio Cordero was one of the most ruthless drug kingpins in South America. He'd kidnapped five of her father's employees in Sanselmo, and killed two of them when the ransom money didn't arrive as quickly as he'd wanted. "What is your brother doing to stay off Cordero's radar? What are the rest of you doing, for that matter?"

"Cordero sent men after my brother and his wife and son last year. *Los Tiburones*—his enforcers. My family and the local cops killed or captured them before they could hurt any of us," J.D. answered. "I guess Cordero realized we won't be so easy to take out. Luke's been sticking close to home, too, not giving Cordero any more easy chances to get to him."

He spoke so calmly, as if a firefight with some of the world's most brutal assassins was just another day in Gossamer Ridge, Alabama. But before she could question him further, there was a knock on the door.

Even though she was closer to the door, J.D. beat her there, putting his solid wall of muscle between her and the flimsy wooden door. Once he peered through the security lens, the tension in his shoulders eased a notch. "Deputy Massey," he murmured. He opened the door and let the investigator in.

Massey's eyes widened as they met Natalie's. He took in the bandaged hands and the casual, almost ragged clothes she'd donned back at the house and quirked one brown eyebrow in surprise. "*You* were the target, Becker?"

She started to bristle, then remembered her earlier conversation with J.D. about her work problems. She forced herself to answer in a neutral tone. "Yes. About ten minutes ago." She told him what she could remember about the incident, gratified to find him taking careful notes as if he intended to look into the case seriously. "It happened so fast, and I wasn't expecting anything like that—I just didn't get a good look at the vehicle. I'm sorry."

"Actually, I can tell you it was probably a Mercury Milan, late model, midnight blue," Massey said.

"Did you find the car?" J.D. asked.

"No, but a blue Mercury Milan was reported stolen about two hours ago outside a residence on Lafayette Road," Massey answered. "Bit of a coincidence, huh?"

"I'd say."

"Devlin's outside checking the crime scene. When Toler and his evidence kit get here, we can start gathering info in earnest." He glanced at her. "Are you sure it was a sound suppressor? Maybe you just thought you heard shots and the thuds on the car were gravel kicking up?"

"I saw the gun. I heard the silencer."

"Well, we'll look. But if they took the care to steal a car, they probably used an untraceable gun."

"I know," she said.

Massey's expression softened. "You okay? Looks like you got banged up a little."

She was surprised by his solicitous tone. She and Massey had never been very friendly. She suspected he thought she'd gotten her promotion for political reasons rather than earning it. "Just scrapes. I'm okay. Could have been a lot worse."

"I don't think you need to go back to your house and stay there alone," Massey murmured.

Natalie glanced at J.D. and found him looking at her in

clear agreement with Massey. As much as she hated to con-
cede the point, they were both right. "I could stay with my
parents tonight. They'll hear what happened by tomorrow at
the latest—you know the grapevine in this town—and wonder
why I didn't tell them sooner. So might as well get it over
with."

Massey turned his attention to J.D. "Still in town, I see."

"Family here, remember?"

"Been doing any trespassing lately?"

"No, sir, not me."

Massey's lips quirked just short of a smile. "I didn't know
you knew Deputy Becker. Should have told me. She owns the
property you were trespassing on, so she could have helped
you work it out."

"Seeing as how she's the one who called the sheriff on me,
that probably wouldn't have helped," J.D. said drily.

Massey cut his eyes at Natalie. "But now you've made
up?"

"It was a misunderstanding," she said.

"Which murder theory did you two decide to go with?"

"We've agreed to disagree," J.D. answered.

Massey crossed his arms over his chest. "Well, if I could
suggest an alternate theory, it seems a little hinky to me
that someone took a shot at killing a second Becker sister
tonight."

"We were just discussing that," Natalie admitted.

"Maybe you should talk to your daddy about that party
he's throwing tomorrow night," Massey said. "If someone's
really gunning for the Beckers, it sure would be tempting to
catch the whole family in the same place at the same time."

The party. She'd forgotten all about the party.

"What party?" J.D. asked.

"It's a fundraiser for Amelia's Grace, a charity for battered
women. Carrie started it a few years ago after her high school
friend Amelia died from a spousal beating. It was already

scheduled before Carrie's murder, and we didn't think she'd want us to cancel it."

"I don't reckon she'd want you to put yourself in any more danger, either," J.D. said.

"I could probably talk Roy into assigning a few deputies to patrol during the party," Massey offered.

Boy, wouldn't her father love that. Patrol cars crawling around his mansion as if it was a crime zone. "I'm not sure my father will go for that."

"Then he probably wouldn't go for armed deputies guarding the guests, either," Massey guessed.

"I'll go armed," Natalie said. "I'll keep an eye out." She'd been considering making a quick appearance and leaving soon after, but if her family was in danger, she had to be there the whole time, on watch.

"I'd offer to go with you," Massey said, "but I'm on call Friday night, too, so I can't be out of pocket that way."

"It's okay," she said, touched by the offer. "I'll talk to my dad. Maybe I can get him to hire some extra security for the party." She rather doubted her father would take any advice she gave him, but it wouldn't hurt to try.

"Toler's probably here by now. I'll go let him and Devlin know what we're looking out for. Then when we're ready to leave, I'll follow you to your folks' house to make sure you get there okay." Massey headed out, leaving Natalie alone with J.D.

He was looking at her, a speculative gleam in his eyes.

"What?" she asked.

"I'm good with a gun."

"Yeah, I believe you established that with the whole 'decimated the South American cartel enforcers' story." She narrowed her eyes. "Are you offering to work security?"

"No, I had something more subtle than that in mind."

Her heart did a little flip. "You want to go as my date?"

His eyes twitched, and he paused a second before answering. "No, that's not exactly what I had in mind."

She tamped down a flicker of disappointment. "Then what?"

"Besides family members, who sees everything that goes on in any wealthy household?"

"The staff," she said flatly, though she wasn't sure she knew where he was going with this train of thought.

"What staff does your family employ?"

"We have a housekeeper, Helen, and Raymond, the gardener. My dad has a driver, Terrence. And it's not exactly full-time staff, but my mom goes to the same caterer, Davina Dreyfuss, whenever she throws a party. Davina's staff helps out with the behind-the-scenes things like setting up and serving, and they've done enough events at my parents' place to be familiar with what goes on there." She frowned. "What exactly do you have in mind?"

He grinned. "Think the party could use an extra waiter?"

Chapter Seven

Back in the day, before he joined the Navy and married Brenda Teague, J. D. Cooper had spent a couple of summers as a waiter at the Gossamer Shoals Country Club. The clubhouse restaurant was a favorite place for parties and events, and he'd served at dozens of them over the course of those two summers.

Of course, that had been twenty-five years ago. He'd been younger and a lot more limber. Plus, nearly three decades of crouching over engines had done a number on his knees, which were already starting to crackle as he walked through the gathered crowd in the ballroom at the Becker estate, balancing a large tray of champagne flutes between his hand and shoulder and praying he didn't drop the tray and make a big scene.

Natalie still hadn't shown up in the ballroom. He was beginning to worry.

The Becker mansion was literally that—an imposing estate with an enormous two-story house situated on the highest ground in the coastal town. According to Natalie, there'd been Beckers in Terrebonne for a couple of centuries. J.D. suspected some ancient Becker ancestor had built the hill from dirt hauled in by the wagonful, just to be certain their ancestral home wouldn't be swept away in a storm surge in the Gulf during one of the coast's frequent hurricanes.

He spotted a small, pretty woman with dark hair and eyes talking to a man in the corner. She looked like an older version of Carrie Gray—at least, the way she'd looked in the photograph that ran in the Terrebonne newspaper after her murder. Must be Natalie's mother, Jeanine. Was the tall, gray-haired man speaking with her Darden Becker?

The man turned, and J.D. sucked in a quick breath, his grip on the tray of champagne glasses faltering, making the crystal flutes plink against each other. Jeanine Becker was talking to J.D.'s father-in-law, George Teague.

"Whatever you do, don't drop those things." Natalie's voice in his ear made him jerk, and the glasses rattled again.

He turned carefully to look at her. She gazed up at him with a bright smile that only made it as far as her eyes. In them, he saw raw tension, and a feral alertness that reminded him of their first official meeting at Millie's bar.

But in every other way, Natalie Becker was a completely different creature. She was dressed in a simple halter dress in a dark bluish-green color. The skirt hit just above her knees, showing off well-toned legs he'd seen just a hint of the night before at her house, before she changed from those snug jeans into her sweats. Her hair was twisted into a sleek coil at the back of her head, making him want to reach behind her and free those cinnamon waves he'd gotten a brief glimpse of the other night. She looked every bit as expensive as she probably was.

He managed not to drop the tray. "You clean up good."

She cocked her head, gazing up at him with a mixture of amusement and alarm. "Umm, thanks?"

He supposed his comment wasn't the most complimentary thing he could have said. "Really good."

She chuckled softly. "You look pretty good in a tux."

He craned his neck. "Tie's too tight."

"Listen—I need to tell you something." A waiter passing

by, empty-handed, distracted Natalie from whatever she was about to say. She turned to call after him. "Dennis?"

The waiter quirked his eyebrows, as if he were surprised to be called by name. "Yes, Miss Becker?"

"Dennis, you used to call me Brace Face in school. I think you can manage Natalie now."

Dennis grinned. "How can I help you, Natalie?"

"Could you take the champagne tray for a little while? I need Mr. Cooper here to help me with something else."

"Certainly." Dennis took the tray from J.D., shot Natalie another grin and walked into the crowd, offering drinks.

"Brace Face?" J.D. murmured.

"Orthodontics were not my friend. But I think it was his version of flirting. Listen, there's a little problem—I just found out how my mother decided to handle tonight's fundraising—"

A series of shouts and gasps broke out in the room, jerking J.D.'s attention to the front entrance.

Where pirates were pouring through the door.

His first instinct was to go for the gun strapped in an ankle holster on his right leg. He was already on the way down to a crouch when Natalie caught his arm. "It's okay," she murmured, tugging him back to his feet. "That's what I was trying to tell you. This is how they're taking the donations."

J.D. watched in dismay as a dozen men in brightly colored pirate garb, accompanied by several pretty women in form-fitting pirate wench dresses, spread out across the large parlor, brandishing cutlasses and demanding booty. One of them headed straight for Natalie, his long, very real-looking sword aimed straight at her heart.

"Don't move," she told J.D. under her breath. "It's okay."

The man stopped just short of her, the cutlass hovering right over her heart. "Your money or your life," he said in a low, menacing voice. But his eyes flashed with amusement, as if he were enjoying some sort of private joke.

"I've already contributed, Hamilton," Natalie replied.

J.D. took a closer look at the pirate. So this was the grieving widower, Hamilton Gray. He was a head shorter than J.D. and elegantly lean. He had stylishly tousled dark hair and murky green eyes in a sharp, vulpine face that made him look far more authentic a pirate than the others who flitted about the crowd like raucous, brightly plumed parrots.

"I suppose you find it unseemly of me to take part in the players of this little charade," Gray said, his eyes never leaving Natalie's face. It was as if he were waiting for her to snap, to show the fire that J.D. saw lurking in her deep green eyes.

Natalie didn't give him the satisfaction. "It was Carrie's idea? The pirates, I mean."

"Exactly." Gray smiled, the flash of white teeth making him look more like a coyote on the prowl than a fox. J.D. could see why Natalie found it easy to imagine the man was capable of murder. He probably was, if J.D.'s instincts were still any good.

But being capable of murder wasn't the same as committing it.

Gray's gaze finally wandered away from Natalie's face, settling on J.D. His eyes widened just a hair, making J.D. wonder if he recognized him for some reason.

But he gave no other indication of recognition, merely cocked his head and asked in a dismissive voice, "Could you find me a glass of champagne?"

J.D. tamped down his irritation and wandered off in search of Dennis and the tray of champagne flutes.

He found the other waiter across the room, perilously close to where his father-in-law was deep in discussion with one of the other guests. He started to take the champagne back to Hamilton Gray himself, but at that very moment, a small, pretty woman with short, dark hair flecked with silver turned around only a couple of feet from him. Her bright, dark eyes widened at the sight of him, and her face broke into a bright smile.

"J.D.!" Lois Teague held out her arms toward him. "What on earth are you doing here?"

With an inward sigh, J.D. put the champagne flute back on Dennis's tray and whispered for him to take a glass to the pirate across the room talking to Natalie. Then J.D. turned back to face his mother-in-law, pasting on a big smile.

"Hi, Lois," he said and stepped into her hug.

"I'VE NEVER SEEN THAT waiter before. Has Davina hired someone new?" Hamilton sipped the champagne Dennis had brought to him, glancing across the room just as J.D. bent to hug Lois Teague. Natalie rather wished she had a glass of champagne herself, but if she wanted to stay alert, she had to limit herself to tea or coffee tonight.

She decided the best way to keep Hamilton from asking questions she didn't want to answer was to tell him as much of the truth as she could. "He's just passing through. I met him the other day at Millie's. He seems nice enough. His son is here in town, visiting his grandparents."

"The Teagues, I presume?"

"Right. Anyway, I mentioned the fundraiser, and he volunteered to help out. I asked Davina if she could use more staffers, and she jumped on it. Especially if she didn't have to pay him." She tried to keep her gaze on Hamilton, but the sight of J.D. deep in conversation with Lois Teague was more of a distraction that she would have expected.

What were they saying? How much of the truth was he telling his mother-in-law?

"I've never known you to pick up strange men in bars, Natalie." Hamilton's eyes seemed to burrow into her brain, as if seeking the tidbits of truth she was hiding from him. She steeled herself against that probing gaze, even as a shudder rippled down her back at the sense of violation.

"You don't know me, period," she said coolly, moving away from him.

"I know you better than you realize," he murmured behind her back, his voice barely audible.

Except for a hitch in her step she couldn't hide, she ignored him and crossed the room to where her parents were talking to a small group of old friends.

J.D.'s gaze snagged hers on the way over. He was now talking to his father-in-law, George, as well as Lois. He seemed to be warning her away with his eyes, so she headed out of the ballroom and into the private family quarters in search of a quiet place to gather her wits after her unsettling encounter with Hamilton Gray.

He seemed to save his psychopathic moments just for her. Was it because she was the only person who saw him for what he was? Or was it something even creepier than that? Could he be targeting her for his next kill? Had *he* been wielding the gun last night at the Bay View Inn?

Her aimless wandering took her into the room her sister, Carrie, had occupied when they were both still kids living at home. Carrie's tastes had always run toward bright, sunny colors and big, bold patterns, inclinations that took charge in her bedroom. The walls were painted buttercup yellow, with bright yellow drapes covering the two large windows on the eastern wall. The bedspread was white, patterned with enormous yellow sunflowers, Carrie's favorite flower.

Fresh sunflowers sat in a bright green vase on the pale beech wood dresser across from the bed. A flutter of pain darted through Natalie's chest as she crossed to the dresser and touched the hardy golden petals. They were still moist and firm, as if they'd been cut just this morning.

"Oh, Mother," Natalie whispered, blinking back tears.

"Your mother cuts fresh sunflowers from the conservatory every day."

Natalie turned to find her father watching her from the

doorway. "I know she misses her terribly." Jeanine had loved both of her daughters, but she and Carrie had been kindred spirits in a way she and Natalie never had been. Carrie's death had been a body blow for her mother.

"I saw you speaking with Hamilton. I hope you gave him no further difficulty."

"I behaved," she answered shortly, trying not to take his veiled scolding too personally. She knew her father and Hamilton's father did an enormous amount of business with each other. Even the slightest misstep on either side could be catastrophic to their companies.

And there was certainly no compelling evidence against Hamilton to point to and prove her theory.

"I wish you had decided to stay longer. Your mother enjoyed having you here last night."

"I needed to feel safe in my own house." She'd called a security company first thing that morning and ordered a rush installation of a security system. They'd installed it this afternoon while she waited, shortly before she had to return to her parents' house for the party.

"Perhaps you weren't the target at all." Something in her father's voice told her that he was speaking a wish more than a conviction.

"Do you know who it could be? Could it have to do with the kidnapping in Sanselmo?"

"Always a possibility. The cartels are getting mean and brave these days, and border security being what it is—"

She nodded, remembering J.D.'s tale of Eladio Cordero's hit squad, who'd made it to Gossamer Ridge just last fall with the full intention of killing as many Coopers as they could. "Did you ever cross the Cordero cartel?"

"More than once," Darden admitted. "Do you have reason to believe they could be behind the drive-by shooting?"

"Do you?"

Darden looked at her, his lips pressed to a thin line. But before he could speak, J.D. appeared in the doorway behind him.

Darden turned at the sound of J.D.'s footsteps. "Yes?"

J.D. glanced at Natalie. "I was looking for Ms. Becker."

Darden gave J.D. a speculative look. "This is the private part of our home. It's off-limits to guests or staff."

"It's all right, Dad. J.D. is a friend of mine." She passed her father and took J.D.'s arm. "Just walk with me," she said under her breath.

They drifted from Carrie's room to the one she'd occupied herself growing up. Compared to Carrie's bright little parrot of a room, hers was more like a quiet sparrow, with its dun-colored walls, rust-brown drapes and simple olive-green bedspread. Her mother hadn't enshrined this room. She'd discovered that fact the night before, when she went to put some of her things in the chest of drawers and found them full of her mother's files—Jeanine took her role as a socialite seriously, claiming membership in a mind-boggling number of boards, commissions and foundations. Her overflowing office had finally exploded into Natalie's old room.

"You disappeared. I got worried." J.D. looked around the room. "Was this your room as a kid?"

"Yeah."

He nodded as if it didn't surprise him. "It looks like you."

She looked around, oddly self-conscious. Considering her earlier thoughts about the room's drab appeal, she wasn't sure J.D.'s assessment was a compliment.

"It's classic," he elaborated. "Simple and straightforward. Doesn't bother pretending to be something it's not."

She quirked an eyebrow. "All that from a bedroom?"

"You're not showy, Natalie. You don't put on airs. Maybe you even try to hide a little bit." He moved closer to her, reaching out to snag a lock of hair that had slipped free of her chignon. He tucked it behind her ear, leaving a trail of electric sparks where his fingers touched her temple. "But quality shows."

She didn't know how to answer such an odd but pleasing bit of flattery. She tried brushing it off with a laugh. "Quality shows, huh? Guess those orthodontic bills and dermatologist visits paid off."

He left his hand on the side of her face, his fingers lightly tracing the curve of her cheekbone. "You look lovely tonight. I hope every person you met told you that."

No one had. No one but him. She hadn't realized until now just how much she'd needed to hear it. "Thank you."

"People are going to start looking for you. For me, too— I've got to be the worst waiter to ever work a party like this." He dropped his hand away from her face, although he seemed reluctant to do so. "I guess we should go back."

She didn't want to leave. She wanted to stay right here in this room where she'd dreamed a thousand dreams and keep talking to J. D. Cooper. Maybe he'd tell her something else nice about herself and make the night even better. "I saw you speaking with your in-laws. How did you explain your presence?"

"I told them I met you the first day I came to town and ended up agreeing to help you look into your sister's murder."

"So you didn't tell them your theory that her murder was connected to Brenda's?"

"Not yet. They still think the murder was solved two months ago. I haven't found the heart to tell them otherwise yet. It'll be hard on them."

Natalie nodded. She knew the Teagues only distantly, even though Lois was a cousin. George Teague was the only general practitioner in town, so most families had been to Dr. Teague from time to time, even if their primary care physicians were located elsewhere. Sometimes, simple scrapes and bruises weren't worth the forty-minute drive into Mobile to see another doctor. Natalie had been patched up by Dr. Teague more than once in her childhood.

"Who's watching your son?" she asked, remembering what he'd told her about the threats against his family.

"Brenda's brother and his wife. Was that Carrie's room— where you were before? Could you take me back to see it?" J.D. asked, catching Natalie by surprise.

She hesitated to answer, not sure what insights he expected to find there. It was just a room. A bright, pretty room that Carrie had once occupied. It was a piece of her, but only a tiny piece. Still, she could tell seeing the room meant something to him. So she nodded and led him next door to her sister's room.

He looked around the bedroom slowly, taking in all the details. Like Natalie, he also noticed the fresh flowers, crossing to touch their petals as she had. He glanced at her. "Your mother?"

She nodded.

He dropped his hand to his side, his lips quirking in a faint smile. "Brenda kept koi in a pond out back. She loved those gaudy, little fish. We kept them thriving for a long time, even after she was gone." His expression darkened. "But one night, a storm blew the protective screen off the pond. A pair of hawks in the woods nearby saw a chance for fresh fish."

She winced. "I'm sorry."

He touched the sunflower petals again. "Sometimes you just can't keep everything safe. All it takes is bad luck, a little inattention and a predator looking for an easy target."

He was talking about Brenda. And Carrie. And all those other women he believed died at the hands of the men who'd murdered his wife. All innocent victims who'd been temporarily vulnerable, in the wrong place at the wrong time.

J.D. turned to look at her. "You're right about your

brother-in-law. I don't know if he killed your sister, but he's creepy as hell."

A flutter of relief darted through her. "Isn't he? Nobody else seems to see it, but my skin crawls when he's around."

He crossed to her side, running his hands down her bare arms, where chill bumps had formed. "You need to be careful with him. I don't know what his game is, but he apparently plans to play it with you."

She could hardly believe what he was saying. So many people had told her she was lashing out because of her anger about Carrie's death that even she'd begun to question her own motives. Validation from someone like J.D., who wasn't the least bit invested in believing Hamilton Gray might be a suspect in Carrie's murder, shored up her flagging confidence more than she'd thought was possible. "I get the same feeling," she admitted.

J.D.'s hands settled on her shoulders, keeping her close to him. His right thumb brushed lightly over the curve of her collarbone, setting off lovely sparks. "Damn it," he murmured.

She smiled nervously. "Damn it?"

He dropped his hands to his sides and stepped away from her. Cool air filled the gap between them, chilling her skin. "Let's get back to the party," he said gruffly, already turning to go.

A soft humming sound in her purse stopped Natalie from following. She opened the clutch bag and checked her buzzing cell phone. The number wasn't familiar, but she took the call, glad for the distraction.

It was Doyle Massey. "There's been another homicide."

Her blood froze. He wouldn't have called her if he wasn't talking about a homicide that resembled her sister's. "Where?"

"Moss Crossing," he answered. "It's pretty fresh. Someone called in an anonymous tip."

She realized J.D. was standing in the doorway, watching

her. She held up her finger to tell him to hold on a minute. "How long ago—an hour? Two?"

"More like thirty minutes," Massey answered. His voice lowered. "This looks a hell of a lot like Carrie's crime scene."

Her first thought was that Hamilton had killed another woman to throw the cops off his track. He somehow snuck out, drove the twenty-minute trip to Moss Crossing and—

The realization hit her with a thud. There was no way Hamilton could have been in Moss Crossing thirty minutes ago, because he'd been standing in the ballroom, talking to her.

Natalie was his alibi.

Chapter Eight

"Why can't we go to the crime scene?" J.D. had chafed through finishing up kitchen patrol after the party while waiting for Natalie to come through with more information. She'd finally come into the kitchen as he and Dennis were helping the other catering company employees pack up the dishes and cutlery for transport, pulling him aside to inform him that Massey had refused her request to get a look at the Moss Crossing scene.

"Because I'm on administrative leave and you're a civilian," she answered flatly, though he could see she was no happier about the situation than he was.

"There's no way I can be sure the crime scene is really a match without seeing it," J.D. growled. "I'm sure Massey's a good deputy, but he doesn't have access to the crime-scene files I do. Not to mention years of studying those files until they rampage through my dreams at night. All he has is what y'all found at Annabelle's. Maybe that would be enough, but probably not."

She looked at him in silence for a second, and he realized just how much he'd revealed about his life over the last twelve years. Even so, she had barely scratched the surface of how lonely and single-minded his existence had really been.

He'd become alienated from his children by the things he couldn't share with them for fear that his own guilt and anger would end up tainting them. His family had joined him on a series of wild-goose chases with fading fervor each time a lead came to its inevitable dead end—they'd answer any call for help, no question, but with the same dread and resigned sadness an alcoholic's family might feel after dragging a loved one out of the drunk tank one more time.

"Could you give me a ride home?" she asked.

The topic change caught him off guard. "You can't go home."

"I already have." She lifted her chin. "I stayed here last night, but I can't hide here forever." She told him about the security system she'd had installed.

He supposed a security system was better than nothing. "Where's your car?"

"I figured the parking would be crazy here already, so I left it at the house and caught a ride with the Blackburns from down the road from my place. But I don't want them to have to wait until I finish up here."

"Okay," he agreed, anticipation fluttering in his gut. He told himself it was the prospect of seeing her outdoor grill again, but he knew better. Sooner or later, he was going to have to face what he was starting to feel for Natalie Becker, and figure out why it was happening now, when the case he'd thought was finally solved had gone hot again.

But not tonight. Tonight, he would stay in the truck, make sure she got inside safely, and leave without lingering. At least, that was his plan.

But so far during his trip to Terrebonne, reality had a bad way of shooting his plans all to hell.

A BLACK-AND-WHITE sheriff's department cruiser sat at the driveway gate outside Natalie's house on the bay, its lights off. As J.D. slowed the truck into the turn, Natalie peered through the passenger window. "There's someone inside."

"Should we stop here or go on?" J.D. murmured.

"Stop here. Let's see what's up." As J.D. put the truck in park and left the engine idling, Natalie opened the door and stepped out of the truck, stumbling a little as her high heels sank into the soft dirt at the edge of the cobblestone drive. By the time she righted herself, both J.D. and Doyle Massey, who'd emerged from the driver's seat of the sheriff's cruiser, were converging on her from either side.

"You didn't turn an ankle, did you?" Massey asked.

"No, I'm fine. Damned heels." She looked up at her fellow deputy, curiosity burning in her eyes. "Has something else happened?"

"No, nothing new," Massey said quickly. "Sorry, didn't mean to scare you or anything. I was just going to see if you had a minute to take a look at some photos. As a corroborating witness, since you were first on the scene of your sister's murder".

J.D. saw he carried a manila envelope tucked under his arm. "Are those crime scene photos from tonight's homicide?"

Massey shot a wary look his way.

"Let him see them," Natalie told Massey firmly. "He's got an alibi for tonight, and he may have important insight regarding both cases."

"Because of that whole serial killer business he was telling me about?" Massey shot another appraising look at J.D. "I did a little checking. Did you know that fellow Dyson they picked up in Millbridge offed himself in jail?"

J.D. nodded. "So they say."

Massey's eyebrows ticked upward. "You're thinking it was murder instead?"

"I don't know what it was," J.D. answered flatly. "All I know is, I talked to Marlon Dyson earlier that day, and he didn't seem the least bit like a man contemplating the end of his life. He was young. First offender. He could have convinced just about any jury that things just spiraled out of control, all because he wanted to be with a girl who barely knew he was alive. I saw him pull that act, and if I didn't know better, I'd have felt a little sorry for him, too."

"Still would've been behind bars for eight to ten years—"

"So he gets out before he even turns forty. I'm older than that, and I'd like to think I have my whole life ahead of me yet." J.D. shook his head. "I just don't buy that the guy I talked to in Millbridge the other day was planning to drink cyanide within twenty-four hours."

"The photos?" Impatience edged Natalie's voice.

"Let's go inside," Massey suggested.

J.D. saw that Natalie had purchased a state-of-the-art security system from one of the best security companies in the business. It wasn't a hundred percent foolproof, but it was better than staying here alone, completely exposed. Massey caught J.D.'s eye over Natalie's head and gave an approving nod.

The view from the front room was as beautiful as J.D. remembered, until Natalie turned on the overhead lights, turning the windows into mirrors. She waved J.D. and Doyle Massey over to the small round table in the breakfast nook just off the kitchen. J.D. took the seat opposite Massey, while Natalie slipped her chair in between them.

Massey handed over the envelope. "These are copies. The originals are in evidence. If Roy Tatum finds out I gave you these—"

"He won't," Natalie assured the deputy. J.D. noticed the look she gave Massey, a combination of wariness and hope. She'd hinted the night before that she didn't really connect very well with her fellow deputies. She thought they were suspicious of her motives for taking the deputy job in the first place. J.D. was beginning to suspect she'd come into the job expecting—and dreading—that the other deputies would treat her differently. Her own tension and defensiveness could very well have created the exact situation she'd wanted to avoid.

Massey was treating her as a colleague this time around, for whatever reason. Maybe seeing her charge hard after a case she wanted to investigate, despite the sheriff's admonition to stay out of it, had proved to Massey that Natalie was serious about being a good law enforcement officer.

Whatever Massey's reasons, Natalie responded to his signs of acceptance, slowly relaxing as she studied the crime-scene photos with the eye of a real investigator.

"There are signs of struggle." Natalie pointed to a fallen lamp in the crime scene photo. "That wasn't true at Annabelle's."

"It's not true of the other crime scenes, either," J.D. said. "It's one of the reasons I believed, for a while, that Victor Logan killed Brenda."

"Did he know her personally or something?" Massey asked.

J.D. nodded. "Once we knew about Logan, we did a little digging. He'd worked as a journeyman mechanic in northeastern Alabama for a while. The trucking company where Brenda did the books was one of the places he'd done work."

"So Brenda would have known him," Natalie said.

"Yeah. I think she might have been surprised to see him waiting by her car after she locked up for the night, but she probably wouldn't have been alarmed. From what I understand, Victor Logan didn't come off as crazy or dangerous."

Massey clasped his hands in front of him and leaned toward J.D. "If your serial killer pair theory is true, how does that change things?"

"I don't think it does," J.D. admitted. "In all the cases I've been looking at all these years, the victim didn't seem to put up a struggle. My best guess, based on what we do know, is that Victor Logan—and Marlon Dyson after him—were like forward scouts or something."

"Softening up the victims, who knew them, so they

wouldn't be on guard when the alpha killer showed up?" Natalie asked.

"That's what I think."

"It's really kind of ingenious. Sick and twisted, sure, but psychologically smart," Massey commented. "I mean, you've got a guy who clearly gets off on the blitz attack—swoop in, wield the knife, bring the blood and the gore, and then get out. That's his signature, not just his M.O., right?"

J.D. couldn't view the murders with the sort of emotional distance needed to appreciate Massey's enthusiasm, but he managed a nod. "Looks that way."

"But that's not the most efficient way to kill. Most blitz killers just deal with that—the pros outweigh the cons for them—but this guy, he's thought ahead. He's recruited some Ted Bundy wannabe and given him a supporting role—Ted Jr. gets to be the point man. He's like a gentleman killer—he prides himself on his charm, his ability to win their temporary trust. Doesn't look like a dangerous guy, so the victims don't treat him like one."

"But they don't know he's just the front man. The feature act is lurking in the wings," Natalie added.

"And he's a *very* dangerous guy," J.D. murmured.

"So what does it mean that there was a struggle this time?" Natalie asked. "Why wasn't he able to win her trust?"

"Who was she?" J.D. asked. Part of him dreaded knowing, because putting a face—a life—to the bloodstained body in that photo added one more scar to his already ravaged soul. But it was the least he owed her—to learn her name and acknowledge her life.

"Her name was Lydia Randolph. She was a nurse practitioner—worked at a low-income clinic in Moss Crossing. A couple of nights a month, she stays late to do inventory—she has to requisition supplies, drugs, that sort of thing from the county hospital, so she has to keep a tight control on her inventory."

"Tonight was one of those nights?" Natalie guessed.

"Yeah."

"Who found her?" J.D. asked.

Massey gave him a pained look. "Her husband."

J.D. felt sick.

"Maybe this guy is having to work solo now," Massey suggested. "It could explain the struggle. The—what do you call it, secondary killer?"

"The beta," J.D. supplied. At least, that's what Gabe's girl-friend, Alicia, called him, and she'd gotten the rest of the Coopers using the same term.

"Maybe there's no beta killer now. The alpha's doing it on his own, and she doesn't have a reason to trust him, so she struggled with him and knocked over the lamp."

"But Carrie didn't seem to put up a struggle," Natalie pro-tested. "There wasn't anything out of place there."

"I've always figured it's not so much that they don't strug-gle—it's that the alpha always cleans up afterward—that's why there's never evidence." J.D. looked at the crime scene photo again. "So the real question is why didn't he clean up after himself this time?"

"You think it's a copycat?" Natalie looked at him, her expression thoughtful.

"I'm not sure what I think," he admitted, almost wishing he hadn't agreed to give her a ride home. He could have done with one more day without dealing with another murder.

"Well, these are yours, Becker." Doyle Massey pushed the envelope of crime-scene photos toward Natalie. "If Tatum finds out you have them, I'm toast. I'm trusting you not to hare off and do something stupid to get us both fired."

Natalie gave him that same wary but hopeful look J.D. had spotted earlier. "Thanks, Massey. I'll be discreet."

Massey looked at J.D. "You heading out now, Cooper?"

"No, I think I'll stay a few more minutes."

Massey glanced at Natalie, who was poring through the

photographs. His lips twitched with the hint of a smile. "Okay. You two kids don't stay up too late. I'll let myself out."

Natalie dragged her attention away from the photos. "Thanks again, Massey."

"Cover my backside, Becker," he called down the hall behind him. The front door opened and he was gone.

Natalie broke the silence a few seconds later. "You don't think it was the serial killer, do you?"

"I meant it when I said I don't know."

Her brow furrowed. "Some of the details match perfectly—the position of the body, for one thing. The situation—night time, all alone in a secluded area—"

"I wish I had my file folder here. I locked it in the motel safe before I left for the party."

She flashed him a rueful smile. "Your experience with me notwithstanding, we're not really a town full of lock-picking snoops. Honestly, around Terrebonne, you could probably leave the files in your truck with the door unlocked and nobody would bother them. They're not valuable to anyone but us."

"Us," he repeated, unable to hold back a small smile.

She shot him a curious look.

He released a soft sigh. "I was just thinking how alone I've been feeling lately."

She cocked her head. "Alone? Surrounded by all that family up in Gossamer Ridge?"

"Yeah, but—" He paused, not wanting to give her the wrong impression of his family. "They've supported me completely. My sister and brothers have pitched in, helped me follow leads. My brother Luke, who was living all the way across the country, looked into a couple of killings in San Diego County for me just because they sounded similar. They went out of their way for me any time I needed help."

"But?"

"How long can you keep going? Twelve years is a forever to keep looking for answers. It wears you out."

"They've given up?"

He stood up, pacing toward the picture windows where his own reflection stared back at him, hollow-eyed and restless. "They've started their own families. Built their own lives. Luke and his wife and kid have prices on their heads, for God's sake. Aaron's got a wedding to plan. Sam's wife just told us she's pregnant with their first child. Hannah and Riley are trying to have another baby, and Jake and Mariah—"

"I get it," she said, her voice close. He turned to find her gazing up at him with gentle understanding. She put her hand on his arm, the heat of her fingers seeping through his cotton sleeve. "And now, there's just you fighting the good fight?"

"I don't begrudge them any of the happiness they've found. I don't expect them to mold their lives around my concerns."

"But you still feel alone."

He was surprised by how much he didn't feel alone at this moment, with her hand warm on his arm and her sharp green eyes gazing straight into his soul. "Not at the moment."

The air between them grew heavy and heated, as if a storm were brewing, thick with unleashed fury. The need to touch her overwhelmed him, until the only way he could quiet the thrumming in his ears was to lift his hands to cradle her face.

Her lips trembling apart, she lifted her other hand to his forearm, her fingers gripping tightly. "J.D.—"

He kissed her before his caution could kick in to stop him. He didn't want to be the careful man, the responsible man that life and circumstance had forced him to be. He wanted to feel something again. Fire. Hunger. Excitement. Even regret. Anything besides the numbing anger, grief and guilt that had driven him for twelve long years.

Natalie responded with feverish ardor, her body pressing

against his, driving him back until his body flattened against the windows behind him. She tangled her long legs with his, the soft heat of her sex cradling his thigh. He felt her soft gasp of pleasure explode against his lips, and his heart began to gallop.

No. He couldn't do this.

He pushed her back, escaping her strong grasp, and retreated a few feet away, turning his back so that he could no longer see her flushed face or her kiss-stung lips.

"I can't," he growled.

"I'm sorry—" She sounded mortified.

He turned swiftly, anger rushing in to feed off the fire of frustrated need. "No. This has nothing to do with you."

She stared at him, her eyes brimming with hurt. But not for herself. "Twelve years of this?"

He knew what she was asking. "More or less," he admitted.

"You still love her that much?"

"I'll always love her that much," he answered simply. The problem was much more complicated than just loving his dead wife, of course, but he didn't want to stand here in the debris field of his screwed-up life and hold a postmortem of how things had gone so terribly wrong tonight.

He just wanted to go back to his motel room where he could lick his wounds in private.

Natalie's silent regard felt like a rebuke, one he knew he deserved. But there was no censure in her wide-eyed gaze, only a dawning understanding. "You blame yourself for her death."

"I didn't kill her."

"That's not what I said."

He hadn't realized how much it would hurt to have the words spoken aloud. Nobody in his family had ever said them. He'd never voiced them to anyone else. It had taken Natalie, a woman he'd met only days ago, to toss the idea into the ether, giving it substance and heft.

"I was her husband. I should have been there to stop it."

Natalie wrapped her arms around herself as if she were cold, although the room was a little warm, the heat from the June day not yet having dissipated. "Where were you?"

"On temporary duty in Groton, Connecticut, working on submarine maintenance for the Navy."

"So you were serving the country," she said, her voice bone dry. "Yeah, I can see why you'd beat yourself up for that. Rather than, you know, blaming the actual killer."

He glared at her, not wanting her easy absolution. "You know damned well it's more complicated than that."

"Yeah, I do," she admitted, looking away.

So, apparently there was more to her story as well. "Where were you the night your sister died?"

"Ignoring her phone calls," she answered bleakly, crossing to the window. She pressed her forehead against the glass pane. "We'd fought about Hamilton earlier that day, and I was so angry."

"Why were you angry?"

She whirled around to face him, tears glittering in her eyes. "She wouldn't leave him. She thought he was having an affair. He was gone all the time, didn't tell her where he was going. He'd stopped wanting to sleep with her—all the classic signs of an affair. But she didn't want to confront him about it."

"How long had they been married?"

"Since this February."

Her answer caught him by surprise "That recently?"

"We've known the Grays for years, but we didn't really socialize that much. Last January, Carrie and Gray reconnected at a charity event in Mobile. Next thing I know—"

"Whirlwind marriage?"

"Yes. I tried to slow her down. I knew it was a bad idea." Natalie rubbed her bare arms. "I was so sure Hamilton was behind her murder, but I don't see how he could be, now.

You're right about the serial killer, aren't you? I've made everyone's life hell for the last few weeks, and for what?"

"I'm not sure you're wrong," J.D. admitted, voicing a realization he'd been trying to ignore over the last couple of hours. "I think the serial killer angle could be a misdirection."

Natalie frowned. "So, you're saying—what?"

"I'm saying I think you may be right. I think it's possible Hamilton Gray killed your sister."

Chapter Nine

Natalie shook her head as J.D.'s words sank in. "But he has an alibi. I know I doubted his first one, but I saw him tonight myself. Several times. No way he had time to drive to Moss Crossing, commit a murder and drive back."

"He could have hired someone to do it for him."

"But why? To cover Carrie's murder?"

"People have killed people at random to cover their tracks before," J.D. pointed out. "As wealthy as your brother-in-law is, he'd have no trouble coming up with a tempting amount of money to convince someone to kill for him."

Natalie pressed the heels of her palms to her forehead, over the throbbing pain that had settled behind her eyes. "I don't know. It's such a convenient answer. Maybe too convenient." She dropped her hands, forcing her gaze to meet his. "Maybe I want to believe it's true because I need someone to blame, and I dislike Hamilton so much."

"I *don't* want to believe it," J.D. murmured. "This whole thing will have been another wild-goose chase for me. But I do think it's possible."

Natalie licked her lips, imagining she could still taste him there. A tremor ran through her, but she stiffened her spine against the resulting weakness. "I think it's late. We've had a hell of a night. And we both are working too hard here to make the evidence fit our theories instead of letting our theories fit the evidence. Maybe we need to take a step back."

J.D. was silent for a moment, but then he nodded. "I should get out of here. Let you get some sleep."

She walked him to the door, tamping down the temptation to ask him to stay. He wouldn't do it, even if she asked, and she knew deep down it wasn't a good idea to get involved, casually or otherwise, with a man who was devoted to another woman.

Even one who was dead.

He turned in the doorway. "I'm sorry things went as far as they did tonight. I knew it was a bad idea and I shouldn't—"

She pressed her fingertips to his lips, silencing him. "You didn't do anything I didn't want, except stop." She managed a wry smile, though her chest was tight with unexpected pain. "And I'll get over that."

"Can we still work together? Because you know more about what happened to your sister than anyone. I need that insider's viewpoint to make sense of all of this."

She nodded. "We can work together. I'd like to take another look at your files. I think we need to start from scratch, look at everything we have without any preconceptions about what happened. Do you agree?"

"Yes." He looked relieved.

"Okay. I'll call you in the morning and we'll figure out where and when to meet." She gazed up at him, wishing she was the kind of woman who could bend a man to her will. Because right now, she couldn't think of a thing she wanted more than for J. D. Cooper to kiss her.

But she wasn't that kind of woman, and he didn't kiss her. He just lifted his hand in a goodbye salute and walked up the drive to where his truck was parked.

She stood in the doorway, watching until his truck disappeared from view down the road. Then she locked up behind her, leaning back against the cool wood of the door.

If your heart gets broken this time, Becker, you have nobody to blame but yourself.

J.D.'S CELL PHONE RANG around eight-thirty the next morning. He'd been up three hours, despite a largely sleepless night, waiting for Natalie's call.

But it was his brother Gabe on the phone. "The Millbridge police are investigating Dyson's so-called suicide, but so far, everything's a dead end. They assumed cyanide from his symptoms right before he expired, but the preliminary tox screen isn't coming up with any of the usual suspects. Nobody at the jail will cop to seeing anything—guards nor inmates—and the jail's video system's a piece of unreliable crap, apparently." Gabe sounded deeply frustrated. He had almost as big a stake in finding the alpha killer as J.D. did, since he still blamed himself for the murder.

"There's been another killing down here," J.D. told his brother.

"Like the rest of them?"

"At first glance, yeah."

"You don't sound convinced," Gabe said.

"I'm not. There were signs of struggle this time."

"Well, we know at least one of the victims here in Millbridge fought with the killer—remember the fingernails?" Gabe said. The victim Gabe himself had found at a Millbridge convenience store the month before had freshly clipped fingernails, leading police to believe the victim had scratched her attacker, who'd then taken care to remove her nails to get rid of any DNA evidence.

"He got rid of the fingernails to keep the cops from identifying him," J.D. said. "But this time, he left a lamp lying on its side, maybe other signs of a struggle."

"He didn't cover his tracks?"

"Exactly." J.D. glanced at the photographs spread across the motel room bedspread. "I'm looking back over the other crime-scene photos to make sure we didn't miss something, but I'm not finding any other signs of a struggle. Which means even if the victims did fight back, the killer took pains to erase any evidence of it."

"So why not this time?"

"That's the big question, isn't it?" A knock on the door dragged J.D.'s attention away from the photos on the bed. He crossed to the door and looked through the security lens. A distorted image of Natalie gazed back at him. "Gotta go, Gabe. I'll talk to you later." He hung up and opened the door.

Natalie's expression was hard to read, but the box in her hand was emitting an amazing aroma of coffee and doughnuts, suggesting she was here on a peace mission, and she'd brought a tasty offering.

"I know I said I'd call first, but—" She stopped, sounding a little flustered. "Have you eaten breakfast yet?"

"Actually, no. Is that coffee and doughnuts I smell?"

She managed a nervous smile. "Yeah. I wasn't sure what kind you'd like, so I got a few different types—crullers and chocolate covered, and there's a cream-filled doughnut that's good enough to tempt a health food nut into sin." She thrust the box at him.

"Come on in." He led the way into the room and set the box on the small table by the window. He opened the top and found two covered cups and an assortment of six doughnuts. His stomach growled, making Natalie smile.

"I'm sorry about last night. I mean, I'm not sorry about kissing you, but I'm sorry it put you in such a bad position."

He found her brash honesty appealing. She didn't seem inclined to hide her feelings from him, whether they were blazing anger, simmering desire or nervous embarrassment. In most ways, she was nothing at all like Brenda had been, but like his late wife, she seemed to put great value on the truth.

"You have nothing to be sorry for. I'm sorry for embarrassing you."

"I've been embarrassed before. I'll live." She shot him another quick smile before turning her attention to the photographs spread out on the bed. "I see you're already at work this morning."

J.D. pulled out one of the coffees and opened the lid. Hot and black, just as he liked it. He took a sip, grimacing with satisfaction as the strong, hot coffee burned down his throat. "I wanted to see if we'd missed any signs of a struggle in previous crime scenes."

"And?" She pulled her own coffee from the box.

"And nothing," he admitted. He waved for her to sit in one of the two chairs flanking the small table and took his own seat. Grabbing a couple of napkins from the stack in the box, he fished a plain yeast doughnut out. It was fluffy and delicious. "Good doughnuts."

"Margo makes them fresh on Saturday mornings. Just Saturdays—she says it's too stressful to come up with that kind of culinary artwork every day." Natalie took the chocolate-topped cream-filled doughnut and took a bite, licking the pale cream from her lips with the tip of her pink tongue. The resulting hunger rumbling through J.D. had nothing to do with food.

He took another sip of scalding coffee and concentrated on the manila folder he saw peeking out beneath the box of food. "What's that?"

She followed his gaze. Her expression darkened. "Photos from my sister's crime scene."

Though his first instinct was to set the doughnut aside and see what was inside that folder, he could see how much Natalie dreaded opening it. He quelled his curiosity and sat a little longer, eating his doughnut in companionable silence.

Natalie picked up a napkin and blotted her lips, reminding J.D. of the second time he'd seen her, drinking whiskey at Millie's. His lips curved. "I bet you went to charm school, didn't you?"

She shot him a curious look. "Yes. Why?"

He shrugged. "You're just such a contradiction—refined but earthy. Polite but forceful. Studious but instinctive."

"Maybe I'm just plain mixed up," she said with a wry smile.

"Who isn't?" His phone rang, vibrating against his leg. He pulled it out and checked the caller. His son, Mike. He answered quickly. "Hey, kiddo. What's up?"

"Just calling." At thirteen, Mike's voice was starting to change, reminding J.D. just how quickly his son's childhood was passing by. He'd already missed so much of it. He should be at his in-law's place, picking up his kid and taking him back home to Gossamer Ridge. They should be spending the day together on the lake, fishing and shooting the breeze, doing the kinds of things other fathers and sons did.

But Mike should also have his mother, and thanks to the bastard J.D. was trying to find, he never would. He tamped down his guilt one more time and schooled his voice so that none of his inner conflict came out in the tone. "What do you and your grandparents have planned for today?"

"Not sure yet—Gran's baking this morning for some deal at church tomorrow, and she's letting me lick the spoon, so I reckon I'll be hanging here for a little while yet." Mike laughed. "When are you getting here?"

"Soon," J.D. answered, hating himself for the partial lie. "Don't eat your grandparents out of house and home, you hear me?"

"Believe me, Dad, Gran's not happy unless she's stuffing something down my throat."

J.D. heard his mother-in-law's chuckle of protest, and his son's laugh in response. His heart contracted. Thank God for the Teagues, and for his own parents back home in Gossamer Ridge. They'd made sure his children grew up loved and protected, even when he couldn't be there. He wasn't sure he could've gotten through the last twelve years without them. "Can I talk to your grandmother a moment?"

"Sure." Mike passed the phone to his grandmother.

"Hi, J.D." Her voice changed color. "What's up?"

"Can you send Mike where he can't hear?"

She put her hand over the phone, muting her voice, but he heard her tell Mike to go see what his grandfather was up to. A second later she came back on the line. "Is something wrong?"

"No. Everything's okay," he assured her. "But I don't want Mike to know I'm here in town yet. He'll have questions I'm not ready to answer."

"Okay." She lowered her voice. "Are you going to tell me what you're really doing in Terrebonne this time?"

He glanced at Natalie. She was busy trying not to watch him, but he knew she heard every word.

"Soon. I should be able to tell you everything in a day or two."

Lois released a soft sigh. "Should I worry?"

"No, you shouldn't worry," he said firmly, hating that she even had to ask. She shouldn't have lost her daughter to a killer, shouldn't be having to send her grandson from the room in order to talk to her son-in-law.

He'd hoped he wouldn't have to tell her that her daughter's killer wasn't dead until the son of a bitch was in custody. But he'd seen the questions in Lois's eyes at the party. Maybe if he told her a little more about his investigation into Carrie Gray's murder, he could erase some of the worry from her eyes. It was the least he owed her.

"Tell Mike I love him and I'll see him soon." He hung up and set the phone on the table in front of him, looking up at Natalie. "I don't know how much longer I can pretend Brenda's murderer died in Mississippi two months ago."

"They deserve to know the truth, even if it hurts."

He pushed aside the box of doughnuts, his appetite gone. "I'm not sure I even know what the truth is."

She put her hand over his, her fingers strong and warm. "So let's find out what it is."

He looked down at her hand, overwhelmed with the desire to turn his own hand over until they were palm to palm. Instead, he gently pulled his hand away.

A faint flush tinting her cheeks, she crossed to the bed to look at the photos. "Where do you want to start?

"At the beginning," he said grimly. "With Brenda's murder."

NATALIE WATCHED J.D. flip through the photographs from his wife's murder scene. As he gave Natalie a terse accounting of the events of that night twelve years ago, the only outward sign of reaction was a twitching muscle in his jaw. But she saw the simmering rage in his eyes each time he glanced her way. "Nobody connected Logan to the murder at the time because he continued to work for the company for a few weeks longer."

"Cold-blooded bastard," Natalie murmured.

"We haven't found another murder in the area that fits the killer's M.O. or signature." J.D. laid the last photograph atop the neat stack he'd made as he told the story. "The next murder we've been able to connect to Brenda's happened almost a year later in Saraland, Alabama." He picked up a photograph and tossed it onto the bed next to where she sat. "Adele Phillips. Age twenty-six. She worked at an auto parts store owned by her uncle. She often worked late in the back office doing the books. She was getting her master's degree in accounting at South Alabama."

He slid another photo toward her. "Vivian Nettles. Age

twenty-seven. Worked two jobs—part time at a Meridian, Mississippi, auto repair shop during the day, and a late-night janitorial job at the local skating rink where she was killed."

One by one J.D. showed her the photos he had. At a glance, they were all similar—pretty dark-haired, dark-eyed women in their mid- to late twenties, fit but curvy. Her sister, Carrie, fit the profile almost perfectly, though at twenty-nine, she'd been at the top end of the profile, age-wise.

"Know what confuses me?" she asked after he'd passed the latest crime-scene photo to her.

He settled on the opposite edge of the bed, sitting so that he faced her. "What?"

"Carrie's murder fits perfectly. No sign of a struggle. No evidence gathered that would help us in the least. But the latest one in Moss Crossing—it just *feels* different, you know?"

He picked up the Moss Crossing crime-scene photo. "I'll be interested to hear what the coroner says about the stab wounds. These look different to me."

She studied the photo more carefully. "They do. I just can't put my finger on why." She reached over and picked up the nearest photo. It was her sister's murder scene. At a glance, Carrie almost seemed to be sleeping peacefully, as if she'd just lain down for a quick nap on the floor of the restaurant kitchen.

But the grievous wounds in her abdomen, staining her yellow blouse crimson, gave lie to the first impression.

She forced herself to look at the photo, study every inch of it, searching for that nebulous something that nagged at the back of her mind. What was different about the bodies?

She looked at the photograph of Lydia Randolph, the nurse practitioner killed in Moss Crossing. Same position of the body. Same bloodstained blouse—

Except it wasn't the same.

"The stab wounds are different," she said aloud.

J.D. scooted closer. "Where?"

She picked up the photo of Carrie and held it up next to the photo of Lydia Randolph. "Carrie has twelve stab wounds. Lydia Randolph has ten. And Lydia's are smaller. Not as much blood. Not as much damage to the blouse—" Her voice stuck in her throat as the full weight of what her sister had gone through hit her like a gut punch.

J.D. didn't seem to notice, his attention focused on the photos. He reached over and picked up several other photographs, comparing them. "All of the others had twelve stab wounds. Lots of tearing. It's part of his signature. Twelve must have some significance to him."

Natalie shuddered, remembering the way her sister's body had looked, lying on the restaurant's kitchen floor. There had been blood. Lots of blood. But there had been more. Internal tissue, ripped from inside her with the force of the stab wounds—

She pushed the image ruthlessly from her head before the nausea roiling in her gut got any worse.

"You okay?"

She looked up to find J.D. watching her, concern in his eyes. "I'm fine," she murmured, willing herself to be so.

"Maybe we should take a break. This is a lot of nasty stuff to have to look at this early in the day—"

"I said I'm fine," she snapped. Immediately she gave herself a mental kick, softening her voice to add, "Really. You're right, it's nasty stuff, but I'm a deputy and I can handle it."

"I know you can. But I wouldn't mind a break."

"You don't have much more time to work through this," she murmured, remembering his earlier phone conversation with his son. "But maybe it would be a good idea to get out of here for a bit."

His eyes narrowed. "You have something specific in mind?"

"I do," she said, even though the mere thought of what she

was about to suggest made her skin crawl and her blood run cold. "I think we need to go back to Annabelle's."

His eyebrows lifted. "You think the investigators missed something?"

"I don't know."

He gave her a look of pure sympathy. "You sure you want to go back there now?"

She wasn't, but it had to be done. And since she was the person who'd been first on the scene the night it happened, she had the best chance of remembering whether or not something was out of place. "Yeah. Let's go back there."

He held out his hand to her. She stared at his large hand for a moment, knowing what would happen if she touched him. Her whole body would turn into one raw nerve, alive with the energy that seemed to spark between them whenever her flesh met his.

Would that be such a bad thing?

Clenching her jaw against the inevitable sensation, she put her hand in his. He hauled her to her feet with as little effort as if she'd been a small child. And her whole body tingled, just as expected, even after he let go of her hand and started to put the photos on his bed back into their folder.

"I'll take these with us," he said, tucking the folder under his arm. "I'd like to compare the scene at Annabelle's to the others in these photos."

Before she could respond, there was a knock on the motel room door. On instinct, she reached into her purse and removed the Glock hidden inside. J.D. pulled his own pistol, a large two-toned SIG Sauer P250 that gave her a momentary twinge of weapon envy. He exchanged a quick look with her and moved to the window next to the door, glancing out.

With a start, he holstered his gun and shot her a bleak look.

"Who is it?" she asked as he crossed to the door, unlocked it and pulled it open.

In the doorway stood a dark-haired boy in his teens, glaring at J.D. with a look of pure fury. "Hi, Dad. Exactly when were you gonna tell me you were in town?"

Chapter Ten

Beneath the anger, J.D. recognized the hurt driving his son's bitter sarcasm. "When I was ready," he said, knowing a lie would only deteriorate the situation further. "How'd you get here?"

"Derek's bike." Mike waved toward a ten-speed parked in front of J.D.'s truck. "Who's she?"

"I get that you're pissed, but that's no excuse for rudeness. This is Natalie Becker. She's helping me with a project—"

"This is about Mom, isn't it?"

J.D. glanced at Natalie, who stood in the middle of his room, her expression uncertain. "Natalie, my ill-mannered son, Mike."

"Hi, Mike." She ventured a smile.

Mike gave a polite nod. J.D. supposed that was better than nothing. "This is about Mom, right?" Mike repeated.

"Yes, but I want more information before I spring it on you or your grandparents." He motioned for his son to come in. "How'd you find out I was here?"

"I overheard Gran and figured it out. I went to Uncle Clay's and mapped the directions here." Mike flashed a look of boyish pride. "I figured you'd be here because everything else is bed-and-breakfast inns. You wouldn't be caught dead in one of those."

Behind J.D., Natalie released a soft huff of laughter. "That's how I figured out where you were staying, too."

"You were looking for Dad?"

"Well, I was actually looking for his motel room," she answered, slanting a quick look at J.D. "And I didn't want him to be in his room, because I wanted to search it."

Mike's dark eyes brightened. "You broke in?"

Natalie glanced at J.D. again, consternation in her eyes. "Yes, but it was very wrong of me."

J.D. held back a chuckle. "I reckon if you can forgive my trespassing at the restaurant—"

"Delinquent!" Mike's grin let J.D. know the worst of his temper had cooled. "Gonna tell me what you're really here for?"

J.D.'s amusement faded. He'd spent a lot of years trying to keep the worst of the details about Brenda's murder away from his children. Cissy was old enough to remember her mother, so it wasn't a surprise that she'd started researching Brenda's murder once she was old enough; but he'd hoped that Mike, who'd been a baby when Brenda died, might be spared that hunger for answers.

He should have known better. Mike was a Cooper, after all. The desire for justice, for answers, was strong in all of them.

"My sister was murdered a few weeks ago." Natalie spared J.D. the need to search for the right words. "Your dad thinks the person who killed your mother may have killed my sister."

"I thought the guy who killed Mom was dead." Mike's eyes grew dark and wide with alarm.

"We all did," J.D. agreed. "But last month, when Uncle Gabe visited your sister, he came across some information that suggests Victor Logan wasn't the only person involved in the murder."

Mike's anger rose again, darkening his cheeks with a deep, red flush. "And you didn't tell me?"

"I needed more information—"

"You think I'm a baby. You think I'm not old enough to deal with this kind of stuff. That's why you keep it from me, right?"

"I keep it from you because I don't want your memories of your mother to be tied up in how she died," J.D. protested.

"I don't remember her at all," Mike protested. "All I know about her is her murder. And you want to keep that from me, too?"

Pain ripped through J.D.'s chest. "Mike—"

Mike grabbed J.D.'s arm. "I need to know who took her from us, too. And I'm old enough to handle it. I promise."

J.D. pulled his son into a swift, fierce hug. "Mike, I swear to you, as soon as I have answers, I'll tell you everything."

"But not now?" Mike's lips thinned with annoyance.

"I don't know that much." He laid his hand on the back of Mike's head, his heart so tangled with love and pain he could barely breathe. "I'm still trying to piece it together—we're not even sure yet that the murders here are connected to your mom's."

"Murders? More than one?" A look of horror, mingled with curiosity, darkened his son's eyes.

"Maybe. We're not sure they're connected at all."

"How can I help you?"

J.D.'s first instinct was to tell his son that the best way to help him was to go back home to Gossamer Ridge and stay far, far away from the investigation altogether. But how would he have reacted to such a suggestion when he was Mike's age?

Not well. And his son was right—he had a stake in what was going on here, whether he knew all the details or not.

"How are you at playing lookout?" he asked.

NATALIE GLANCED BACK at J.D.'s truck as they approached Annabelle's front entrance. Mike sat in the passenger seat, fiddling with his cell phone. "Are you sure we should leave him in the truck alone?"

"He's not a baby," J.D. said with a slight smile.

She glanced back again. "I'm glad Carrie didn't have any children. Losing a mother so young is a lot to deal with."

His smile faded. "I was lucky to be surrounded by family."

The door of Annabelle's loomed in front of her. Natalie pulled the keys from her purse and unlocked the door, her stomach churning with anxiety. With a little push, the door creaked open, and Natalie forced herself to take a step inside.

After weeks of neglect, the place smelled musty. Natalie also thought she could detect the faint metallic odor of blood.

Her imagination. She'd had a crew come in to clean the place after the police released the crime scene. It was a sense memory, from the night she found her sister.

She'd smelled the blood first, before she found the body.

"Your sister had done a lot of work here?" J.D. asked, his voice jarringly loud in the hushed restaurant, even though he'd spoken in a low tone.

She looked up at him. "She was finishing up with the renovations, about to start hiring staff, when this happened."

Looking around, she tried to view the place through his eyes, without the context of her relationship with Carrie. She noted the solid quality of the dark wooden chairs and tables, a reminder that for all of Carrie's bright frothiness, she'd possessed an underlying core of hardy sensibility.

"Sunflowers," he murmured, pointing to the enormous mural on the far wall.

Natalie followed his gaze to the wall, where the outline sketch of a sunflower filled almost the entire area. Carrie's idea was to rename the restaurant Sunflower and serve fresh, local food only. She had plans to plant sunflowers in the patch of ground out front where a line of aging boxwoods now grew, letting them set the tone of the restaurant—bright, sunny and vibrant with life.

She'd have made a success of this place. Natalie was convinced of it. Carrie knew how to make people feel at home.

The burning sensation behind her eyes made Natalie focus her attention on the job. *Be an investigator, not a sister. Just for a little while. Then you can go home and fall apart.*

"I don't see any sign of a struggle in here," J.D. said.

"I don't, either," she agreed, her gaze settling on the swinging door at the far side of the room. The kitchen entrance.

J.D.'s large hand flattened low on her back, a steadying touch that sent a sudden flood of warmth coursing through her body, as if a portion of his own solid strength had flowed into her through his fingertips.

With a bracing breath, she headed for the kitchen.

The door swung open with only a slight touch of the push plate, the sprung hinges offering little resistance. Once she and J.D. stepped into the kitchen, the door swung back with a soft *whoosh,* rocking quietly until it finally fell still.

She kept her gaze at eye level for a moment, not yet ready to see the floor near the back of the kitchen where her sister had bled out from her stab wounds. Instead, she scanned the room, looking for any signs of a struggle.

"What's with the extra stuff?" J.D. waved toward the stockpile of kitchen appliances. Unlike the dining room, which had been neat if a little dusty, the kitchen was cluttered and chaotic, filled with extras of everything. She had asked the cleaners to only deal with the blood, impressing on them the importance of not moving anything out of position. Keeping the crime scene intact had seemed important, somehow, even though the police had released it.

"Carrie was replacing the old appliances with newer, state-of-the-art appliances," Natalie answered. "But she didn't just want to throw out good, working equipment, so she was checking around with local charities to see who would put them to the best use." The stinging behind her eyes grew stronger. "That's the way she thought. What would do the most good. And now, who'd want it? It was once covered with her blood."

J.D.'s hand found its way to the base of her spine again. Her body leaned toward him, steel to his magnet, and her grip on her emotions slipped, tears burning her eyes. She choked out a brittle sob.

J.D. wrapped his arms around her, his chest warm and solid against her back. Leaning her head back against his broad shoulder, she struggled with her grief. "I'm sorry."

"Don't be." His warm breath stirred her hair.

She hadn't cried since that night, she realized. Not during the wake, not at the funeral, not even at the private graveside service afterward. Her mother had fallen apart from the beginning, and even her father had grieved in his self-contained way, as she'd discovered after the funeral when she'd walked in on him crying alone in his den.

But until this moment, she'd held her own emotions sternly in check, concentrating instead on delivering justice. Finding who'd done this. Making sure he paid.

Pent-up pain and rage poured from her in a torrent of sobs and tears until she felt as if she were coming apart. But J.D.'s arms pinned her together, keeping her somehow intact with gentle caresses and whispered words of comfort, until her tears slowed to a trickle and the sobs faded to soft, hitching breaths.

J.D. stroked her hair away from her damp cheeks. "I bet you've held that in for weeks, huh?"

She nodded, her temple brushing against his beard stubble. The sensation was strangely pleasant. "I guess that's why I've avoided coming in here again."

"We can leave."

"No." She pulled away from his grasp, turning to face him. Threading her fingers through her hair, she pulled the unruly mess out of her eyes so she could level her gaze with his. "Let's do this now so I don't have to come back again."

He brushed her cheek with the lightest of touches. "What do you want to do?"

She made herself look at the floor, where bloodstains had once spotted the tiles. "I found her here." She gestured toward the floor, where her sister had lain wedged between the base of the old stove and the newly purchased high capacity freezer that would have gone on the far wall eventually. "She was lying on her back. Palms on the floor. Her feet were together and her skirt was in place, covering her thighs to the tops of her knees." She shuddered but forced herself to finish. "The coroner said she'd been raped, but he didn't retrieve any DNA evidence."

She could tell by the look on J.D.'s face that he was picturing his wife lying in a similar position. He hadn't been the one to find her, the way Natalie had found Carrie, but she knew he'd spent the last twelve years poring over the crime-scene photos until he had them memorized.

"When was the last time you'd been here, before that night?"

She rubbed her face, trying to remember. "Maybe a couple of days? It was a Thursday night when she died, and I think I'd come by on Tuesday because she wanted to show me the new appliances."

"Did the place look like this?"

She looked around bleakly. "I think so. It was cluttered, but not really messy."

J.D. gave the room a quick scan. "Cluttered like now?"

She nodded. "I looked around for signs of a struggle the night I found her. I think I went into deputy mode out of self-preservation." She sighed. "There was nothing obviously out of place, J.D. I looked. As crazy as it sounds, I know I'd have noticed if there was."

He brushed his knuckles against her cheek. "Okay."

She fought the urge to lean into his touch. "We probably need to see the Moss Crossing crime scene to be sure, but that one just feels different to me. Like two separate people committed the crimes, despite the surface similarities."

He let his hand drop to her shoulder and drew her with him to the swinging door. As they left the kitchen behind them, the air seemed to lighten. She took a breath and let it go slowly.

J.D.'s fingers tightened on her shoulder. "I know this was hard for you, but I really needed to see this place myself. Thank you for bringing me here."

Unable to fight herself any longer, she stepped closer to him, until she felt the heat of his body radiating against hers. "You're welcome."

He slid his hand around the back of her neck, his touch gentle but commanding. Gazing down at her with desire-darkened eyes, he seemed to fill every inch of the world around her until everything else disappeared. Time stretched, expanded, until she lost all track of it.

He lowered his head slowly, his breath burning her lips. So close, so fiercely tempting. His hesitation seemed deliberate, as if to give her time to stop him.

But she didn't want to stop him.

J.D.'s lips brushed hers lightly, then drew away. Blood roared in her ears, drowning out all but need.

She kissed him back, taking her time. Their first kiss had been a mindless frenzy, but she needed something different this time. Something deeper. Something deliberate.

Roping one arm around her waist, he pulled her flush to him. She dropped her hands to his sides, sliding her fingers under the hem of his T-shirt until they met the corded muscles of his rib cage. Beneath the hot velvet of his skin, he was steel-hard sinew, surprising for a man as large as he was. She moved her hands upward, tracing a path across the ridges and planes of his body until his breath exploded in a gasp against her lips.

His fingers tangling in her hair, he drew her face up to his for a kiss that sent the whole world reeling around her in a dizzying rush. Only the smallest vestige of good sense remained to hear the soft snick of the restaurant entry door opening behind her. But it took a couple of seconds for her sluggish reflexes to respond. By the time she and J.D. scrambled apart, it was much too late.

Mike Cooper stood in the doorway, staring at them with a look of pure, adolescent horror.

Chapter Eleven

Well, hell.

J. D. Cooper watched Mike's expression go from mortification to surly displeasure and didn't have one damned clue what to do about it. He'd never put his kids in the position to see him with a woman before. He didn't date, never brought women home to meet the family, and the few times he'd given into the demands of his body over the years, it had been far away from home, with women no more interested in a long-term relationship than he was.

He took a couple of steps toward his son, hoping he could stumble onto the right way to handle the uncomfortable situation. Mike took a defensive step backward, his expression darkening.

"I saw someone in the woods. You said to let you know if I saw anything." Resentment burned in his dark eyes. "I knocked."

"You saw someone outside?" Natalie asked.

Mike shot her a baleful look. "He had a rifle, I think."

J.D. exchanged a quick glance with Natalie, discomfited to find that she looked as tempting as sin, with her tousled cinnamon hair, her cheeks full of color and her kiss-stung lips. "Rudy?" he asked in a hoarse growl.

She nodded.

"It's probably a guy named Rudy Lawler," he told Mike. "He hunts for wild pigs in the woods out there."

"I think I'll just take the bike and head back to Derek's house," Mike said, already heading out the door.

J.D. gave Natalie an apologetic look and followed his son outside. "Mike, you can't be riding around by yourself."

"Cordero probably doesn't even know who I am. He's after Uncle Luke, not you."

"He's after any of us he can get to."

Mike shot a wild look back at the restaurant. "I sure don't want to stick around here."

"Mike, what you saw—"

His son glared up at him. "If I'm going to get a new mom, just tell me that, okay? You don't have to hide her from me."

His son's words stabbed him in the center of his chest, right in the place where he kept all his fears and regrets. "You're not getting a new mother. No one will ever replace your mother, do you understand? Not for you and definitely not for me."

Mike's gaze shifted somewhere behind him. J.D. turned and saw Natalie standing a few feet away, stone-faced and still. He knew she'd heard what he'd told his son, though he couldn't tell from her frozen expression exactly what she felt about it.

Hell, he didn't even know what he felt about what he'd said. Had it even been the truth? When this was over, was he just going to be able to walk away from Natalie with no regrets the way he'd done with other women?

"My parents' house is just a half mile from here, on the other side of the woods," she said aloud, her toneless voice offering him no clue of what she was feeling. "My mother's driver can shuttle me back to the motel to pick up my car."

"You can't walk through the woods by yourself," he said flatly. Her eyebrows notched upward, and he added, "Someone's already tried to kill you once."

"It might have been random," she said, although he knew she didn't believe that any more than he did.

"Someone tried to kill her?" Mike asked, his anger faltering for a moment as fear took over. "You think it could have been the guy who killed Mom?" His eyes widened more. "Or Cordero?"

J.D. squeezed Mike's shoulder. "We don't know. It's why I want you to stay safe at your grandparents' house for a few more days, just until we get a better handle on what's going on."

"What if you don't know what's going on in a few days?" Anxiety threaded through Mike's voice. "Are you going to stay down here until you know?"

"No, of course not," J.D. answered quickly.

"So you're just going to leave town while there's someone trying to off your girlfriend?" Mike asked with blunt candor.

"She's not my girlfriend," J.D. answered defensively.

Mike shot him an incredulous look. "She can hear you, Dad."

J.D. turned and found Natalie watching him through narrowed eyes. He couldn't read her feelings in her masklike expression, which wasn't exactly comforting. He knew she hid her emotions the best when she was feeling most vulnerable. But he'd couldn't unsay the words. And they were true, weren't they?

She wasn't his girlfriend. They weren't going to live happily ever after, no matter how many hot, sweet kisses they shared. Sooner or later, he'd have to go back home. She would stay here. It was just how things were.

"Let's go back to the motel, okay?" he suggested. "I need to get you back to your grandparents' house, and I'm sure Natalie has other things she'd like to do with her day."

Mike eyed Natalie as he climbed into the truck, as if he

were trying to read her mood. Apparently, he wasn't having any more luck than J.D. was.

Natalie climbed wordlessly onto the bench seat at the back of the truck's cab, leaving the front passenger seat for Mike. Wary, J.D.'s son took his place in front of her. The minute J.D. started the truck's engine, Mike began fiddling with the radio dial, finally settling on a rock station out of Mobile.

The short drive back to the motel was uncomfortable but uneventful. Both Mike and Natalie piled out of the truck at the motel as if eager to be shed of J.D. altogether.

"I'll call you later?" J.D. ventured as Natalie started toward her car without bothering with any formal goodbye.

"I'll call you," she tossed over her shoulder without looking back. The "when hell freezes over" part of her sentence was clearly implied in the angry energy that took her across the parking lot in a few economical strides.

"She's not going to call you," Mike murmured.

He looked at his son. "Yeah, I know."

"Did I mess things up for you?"

"I think I managed that on my own," he answered, unnerved at the sight of Natalie driving out of his life, probably for good. How had he let the relationship between them become so important to him so quickly?

He looked away from her disappearing taillights and turned to his son. "You want to grab some lunch in town?"

Mike shook his head. "I promised Aunt Judy I'd be back for lunch. Uncle Clay's grilling steaks. You want to come? Uncle Clay's always saying how he never sees you when you come to town."

The last thing J.D. could handle at the moment was an afternoon with Brenda's brother. "I'll drop by to see everybody later. Maybe tomorrow." He hustled Mike back into the truck.

As he buckled up, Mike released a deep sigh. "I'm not mad at you for kissing her, you know. I mean, I *was,* 'cause—ugh."

He grimaced. "But I know Mom's gone and she's not coming back. Cissy knows it, too. She's been saying for years that we should be glad if you meet someone who makes you happy."

J.D.'s aching heart dropped a beat. "She said that, huh?"

Mike nodded. "So it's okay, you know? If you really like her, then it's okay to kiss her and stuff."

J.D. couldn't decide whether to smile at his son's awkward blessing or kick himself for already rendering it pointless. "Duly noted." He gave his son's dark hair a quick ruffle.

Mike grimaced again and ducked out from under J.D.'s hand. "Dad, do you have to do that?"

This time, J.D. managed a grin, ruffling Mike's hair again. "Yeah, I do. Just to hear you squawk." He started the truck engine and turned down the radio.

Mike protested, and J.D. let him turn it back up, filling the cab with the driving beat of an old Aerosmith song. The loud music and his son's air drums routine precluded any further conversation, but J.D. was okay with that. He and Mike were okay, and that's what mattered.

He just wished the same were true of himself and Natalie.

"You going to eat your fries?"

Natalie looked up from her barely touched lunch plate to find Travis Rayburn standing next to her table. He was smiling at her, though the humor didn't quite reach his watchful eyes.

She pushed the plate toward him. "Knock yourself out."

Travis pulled out the chair opposite her and sat, picking up one of the fries. "How long do you reckon you're going to be on administrative leave?"

"Tatum hasn't said yet."

He grimaced. "Tatum needs to have his head examined. Bill Donovan's still out from his bypass surgery, and Toby

Ellison broke his ankle on an animal nuisance call yesterday. We're three men down now. The least Tatum should do is let you come back on desk duty. Free up someone else to get out in the field."

Natalie gave him a speculative look. "Things are that busy?"

"We're having a big meth problem in the western part of the county. Tatum's created a task force with the DEA to try to figure out who's supplying the pseudoephedrine to the meth chefs. DEA thinks it might be a reputable drug source with something going on the side. We're not so sure. Tatum thinks some of the local dealers are hiring teams of teenagers to lift the stuff from drug stores." Travis shoved the fry into his mouth.

"Don't you have to get that stuff from behind the pharmacy counter these days?"

Travis shrugged. "Send a cute girl in a crop top into any store in the county and I bet you could distract the pharmacist long enough for someone to sneak in the back and lift what they need." He picked up another fry. "Sure you're done with these?"

She nodded. "So Tatum's really shorthanded, then?"

"Everybody's working extra shifts to get things done. Weekends, too." Travis cocked his head. "It's a good time to hit Tatum up for your shield back. If you really want it back."

"Oh, I want it back," she assured him.

Anything to get her mind off J. D. Cooper.

"Well, go talk to Tatum. He was in the office last I saw." Travis reached across the table for the bottle of ketchup by the napkin holder.

"On a Saturday?" she asked, surprised. The sheriff usually had weekends off unless there was an emergency.

"Shorthanded, remember?" Travis finished drowning the fries in ketchup and set the bottle back where it came from.

"By the way, where are you on your investigation of your sister's murder?"

"What investigation?" she asked innocently.

He grinned at her. "Right. You're following Tatum's rules to the letter, I bet."

"You know me," she murmured, smiling. "I'm a to-the-letter kind of girl."

His grin broadened. "Devlin said he saw you with some guy at your folks' party."

"Devlin was there?" Dusty Devlin was one of the newer recruits at the Sheriff's Department. About as green as early corn and the last person she'd have expected to see at her parents' ritzy fundraiser.

"He picks up security jobs now and then for extra money," Travis said. "Got a kid with some medical issues and the bills are hard to deal with."

"I didn't know that." She was beginning to wonder just how many things she didn't know about her fellow deputies—and whose fault that really was.

"Anyway, he said he saw you leave after the party with one of the waiters or something?"

"Right. He's a friend."

Travis's dark eyebrow arched. "A Becker dating the help? Bet that went over great with your dad."

"I didn't say we were dating," she protested, though the memory of J.D.'s hot, sweet kisses didn't exactly add the right level of conviction to her denial.

Travis picked up on that fact. "Uh-huh."

"He's only in town a short time. There's nothing going on." Not after today, anyway. J.D. had made that much painfully clear.

"Well, good. So you won't mind taking time away from him to put in some hours at the station." He waved toward the door. "Get a move on, while Tatum's stuck at the office trying to keep all the balls he's juggling in the air."

Natalie pulled a twenty from her purse and laid it on the table. "Make sure Margo gets that. And buy yourself a Coke before you choke on the fries."

Travis was right; Roy Tatum was still at his desk, eating a cold ham sandwich and working his way through a stack of paperwork so high that he could barely see over it when Natalie entered his office. He looked harried and angry. "What do you want, Becker?"

"I hear you're shorthanded."

"And you want me to put you back on active duty?"

She knew she had to tread lightly here. Tatum was generally a fair man, but he didn't like to be pushed. "I thought maybe I could trade administrative leave for desk duty."

Tatum slanted her a considering look. "You been staying away from your sister's case?"

"Yes," she lied.

The look he shot her way left her with little doubt he saw right through her. But when his eyes dropped back to the stack of papers in front of him, he released a frustrated sigh. "Okay. Desk duty. And you'll be pulling six days a week until we find a temporary replacement for Ellison. He'll be back later next week on desk duty, too, so maybe the two of you can work your way through some of the quarterly expense reports we have to turn into the county treasurer by the end of the month."

She managed not to grimace. Expense reports weren't high on her list of interesting duties. But at least she'd have her shield and weapon back. It was a start.

And she'd also have access to all the Ridley County Sheriff's Department case files dating back to the middle of the last century. Now that she'd seen J.D.'s files and knew what she was looking for, she could scour the cold-case files every chance she got to see if there were any more murders that matched the signature and M.O. of her sister's death.

"Thank you," she said aloud. "I can start now if you want."

He gave her an exasperated look but unlocked his desk and brought out her badge and Smith & Wesson service pistol, still in its holster. "I knew you'd be back here hounding me sooner rather than later," he muttered gruffly.

She smiled. "You won't regret this." She clipped the badge and holster to the waistband of her jeans, hurrying out of the sheriff's office before he had a chance to change his mind.

She ran into Doyle Massey in the bullpen. He didn't look surprised to see her. "Let me guess. You heard about Ellison's broken ankle and figured it was your chance to worm your way back on the force?"

She took a seat at her desk, which was across from Massey's. "I'm a team player, Massey. You know that."

Massey grinned at her. "Y'know, Becker, I think you just might be after all."

His open show of friendliness was a surprise, but it also went a long way toward taking the edge off her black mood. It couldn't fix the mess her personal life had become ever since she'd spotted J. D. Cooper at the cemetery a few days earlier, but at least things were looking up professionally.

She'd take whatever good news she could get.

NATALIE ENDED UP working all day Sunday as well, helping the team catch up on all the paperwork that had started falling behind and getting the preliminary expense report ready to give to the sheriff on Monday for his feedback. But the pace wasn't so hectic that she didn't get a chance on Monday morning to snoop through the old cold-case files stored in the Sheriff's Department annex.

She pulled three files that looked interesting—one murder there in Terrebonne, one over in Otter Bluff and a third in Surrey near the county line, all taking place within the last twelve years. On Monday morning, with the preliminary expense report safely on the sheriff's desk, she finally got a chance to study the files more carefully.

The oldest case, from the town of Surrey, she eliminated outright once she read between the lines and realized the killing seemed to be drug related. A second she moved aside once it became clear that the woman had been merely passing through Otter Bluff and had been killed in a blitz attack; that was the wrong M.O. and nothing like the alpha killer's signature.

That left the Terrebonne case. It had happened just a few weeks after Brenda Cooper's November murder. Three days after Christmas, twenty-six-year-old Carol Freemont had been house sitting for a friend on Hoke Island when someone killed her.

The crime-scene photo showed her lying on the floor of the detached garage, near her dark blue Chevrolet sedan. The car's alternator had been tampered with, ensuring the car wouldn't start if she tried. The lead investigator, Danny Chisholm, had noted in the file that he had contacted every garage and shade tree mechanic in town to see if Carol had called in a request for service. He'd also checked area towing companies to see if she'd called for a tow. None of the inquiries had panned out. But Chisholm hadn't known to look for a connection to Victor Logan.

Natalie reached for the telephone to call J.D. If anyone knew whether or not Victor Logan had been in this neck of the woods at the time of Carol Freemont's murder, J.D. would.

But she stopped herself, replacing the phone on the hook. Not once in the past three days had J.D. contacted her, not even to make sure no one had taken another shot at mowing her down in a parking lot somewhere. So what if she'd told him she'd call him instead? Why did men have to take everything so literally?

She looked around the bullpen, frustrated to find the place empty. A glance at the clock told her why—it was past time to take a break for lunch. She wasn't particularly hungry, but she'd been deskbound for hours, so she shrugged on her lightweight blazer and started for the door.

Travis Rayburn headed into the bullpen just as she reached the door, almost crashing right into her. He was carrying a large black vase full of enormous yellow sunflowers.

Natalie sidestepped him to avoid a collision. "Got a secret admirer, Rayburn?"

Travis grinned at her over the bright yellow flowers. "I was going to ask the same thing—they're for you."

Her smile faded. "From whom?"

Rayburn shrugged. "The card didn't say."

"Who delivered them?"

"They were left outside the back door of the station. I saw them as I was coming in."

That was odd, Natalie thought. She followed Travis back to her desk, waiting for him to set the vase on her blotter before she checked the note.

He was right. It was just a plain white card, tied to the flowers with an equally white ribbon. No illustration, no florist's logo. Her first and last names were digitally printed onto the card in a simple font.

Her stomach began to ache, driving away any thought of hunger. "Sunflowers were my sister's, Carrie's, favorites," she murmured, brushing her fingertip over the bright golden petals of the nearest bloom.

"What are you saying?" Travis asked.

She looked up at him. "I think these flowers are from her killer."

Chapter Twelve

Two days, and she still hadn't called.

J.D. had known she wouldn't. No woman with a shred of self-respect would ruin her parting shot that way. And he'd be damned if he'd call her when she told him not to. Only a pathetic loser or a psychopathic stalker would do something like that.

Still, as he pushed his half-eaten burger around the plate, he couldn't help wondering what she was doing right now.

"Didn't like the way I cooked it?"

He looked up to find Margo looking at his unfinished lunch. "No. It's great. I guess I just wasn't as hungry as I thought."

Margo cocked her head. "Did you ever find what you were looking for?"

He met her gaze, wondering just how much she knew about what he'd come to Terrebonne to find. He wouldn't be surprised if she knew everything, up to and including what had happened between him and Natalie on Saturday at Annabelle's. Margo was the kind of person who could coax state secrets out of a spy. "I'm not sure I'll ever find what I'm looking for," he answered, hoping it was cryptic enough to cover whatever she knew.

"I heard you worked a party up at the Becker's."

"I helped out."

"Odd, doing something like that when you're just here in town for a few days."

"Seemed like the party was for a good cause."

"Natalie Becker tell you about it?"

And we reach the point of this interrogation, J.D. thought. "She did, but working the party was my idea."

"I imagine it was quite the fancy do."

"It was very fancy," he said carefully, considering what he could tell her to appease her curiosity without revealing anything the Beckers wouldn't want spread far and wide. "The party was raided by pirates."

Her eyes widened with interest. "Pirates?"

He told her about the bit of playacting to make donation request more entertaining for the partygoers. "They were dressed to the hilt. Cutlasses and eye patches and good-looking women dressed like bar wenches. There was even a pirate with a real parrot. I had to clean up after the damned thing all night."

"The pirate or the parrot?" Margo asked through delighted laughter.

"Both," J.D. answered with a grin.

"I guess it must have raised quite a bundle of cash for poor Carrie's charity," Margo said, her laughter fading.

"That's what I heard."

Margo slanted a knowing look at him. "Did you hear it straight from Natalie Becker herself?"

Before he could figure out how to answer without starting more tongues in town wagging, the bell over the diner door tinkled, heralding a new customer.

"Speak of the devil," Margo murmured, her gaze moving to the doorway.

J.D. turned and found Natalie standing just inside the door, looking his way with wary eyes.

He tried a smile. She didn't return it, but she did start walking toward him, her pace unhurried.

He stood to greet her. "Hi."

He saw her gaze dart behind him. Margo, no doubt, watching with her usual hawk-like interest. He didn't care.

"Hi," she answered after a moment.

"Can I buy you lunch?" he asked.

Her eyes narrowed slightly. "No, I can buy my own. Margo—my usual please?" Her tone softened as she looked back at J.D. "But if you want to join me, that would be fine."

"Okay." He turned to find Margo holding out his half-finished plate. Biting back a grin, he took the plate and grabbed his glass of tea and joined Natalie at a table near the window.

They sat in uncomfortable silence for a few minutes. Finally, Natalie cleared her throat. "Did you work things out with Mike?"

"Oh, yeah," J.D. assured her quickly. "He just had to get past the whole ick factor."

Her lips quirked. "I didn't even think about that."

He leaned toward her. "I'm glad I ran into you. I've been thinking about you—I don't like the way we left things."

"It's okay. I mean, nobody said anything that wasn't true—" She fell silent as Margo approached with a turkey sandwich, a bag of pretzels and a glass of water. "Thanks, Margo."

"Can I get y'all anything else?"

"I'm good," J.D. said, trying not to sound impatient.

After Margo left, Natalie started picking at the sandwich, but J.D. noticed she wasn't really eating. "Is something wrong?"

She looked up at him. "I don't know."

Alarm wriggled in his gut. "Has something happened?"

"Did you hear I'm back at work?"

"No," he answered, surprised. "Full time?"

"In terms of hours, yes." She stopped pretending any interest in her lunch. "But I'm on desk duty only."

"Well, that's better than twiddling your thumbs at home,

right? At least you have access to the sheriff's department resources—files and the computers—"

"I found another possible murder. Right here in Terrebonne, just a couple of months after your wife's murder." For the first time since she entered the diner, he saw a little light in her eyes. He listened patiently as she outlined what she knew about a murder victim named Carol Freemont. From what she described, she had ample reason to think the murder might be connected to the other murders he'd been tracking for over a decade.

"Good catch," he murmured. "Have you discussed it with Doyle Massey yet?"

"He was out of the office—I found it right before I broke for lunch."

"Is that why you're not hungry?" He gestured at her nearly untouched plate.

She looked down at the plate. "Oh." She picked up half of the sandwich and got it halfway to her mouth before she put it back on the plate and leaned forward. She spoke in a hushed tone. "Someone left me flowers anonymously." She gave him a meaningful look. "Sunflowers."

His gut tightened. Her sister's, Carrie's, favorite flower.

"No return address, no florist's logo, nobody knows how it came to be sitting on the sidewalk outside the sheriff's department front door."

"No video surveillance of the area?"

She shook her head. "Just inside the building for interrogations and that sort of thing. Not outside the building."

"You think the killer left it for you."

"Don't you?" she asked.

He sighed. "I don't know. I can't make sense of anything. First someone tried to shoot you. Now someone's sending you flowers anonymously. It seems a little anticlimactic—"

"It's creepy," she admitted. "Someone trying to shoot me

was scary, but it was—I don't know—businesslike, you know? This is more—"

"Personal?"

"Yes. More personal."

That's what he was beginning to fear himself.

"Maybe we really are looking at two different sets of murders here," she said softly. "Maybe Carrie's was an intentional copycat of the killer you're looking for."

"And what about the Moss Crossing murder? That seems even more like a copycat killing than your sister's murder."

"I don't know." She winced with frustration. "The more I learn, the more questions I have."

He reached across the table and laid his hand over hers without thinking. Her gaze snapped up to meet his, and he withdrew his hand. "Sorry."

She stared at him for a long moment, then reached over and caught his hand in hers. "When I found the old murder file, I wanted to call you so badly."

"Why didn't you?"

She let go of his hand. "You know why."

Heat burned the back of his neck. "Natalie, I'm sorry for what I said."

"You're only sorry I heard it."

"No, I'm sorry I said it. It was an easy answer to give my son so he'd stop feeling freaked out. But it didn't tell the whole truth, did it?" He didn't know why he wasn't taking the easy way out now. All he had to say was that he was in no position in his life to get involved with a woman. That was true, wasn't it?

"It told enough of the truth," Natalie murmured. "I'm not your girlfriend. You're not sticking around here that much longer, so anything between us is temporary. I know that."

"If things were different—"

"They're not," she said flatly. "But I need your knowledge, and you need my access to the police files. So I say we put aside the awkwardness and just deal with each other like professionals."

He wasn't sure he was capable of being strictly professional with her. She got under his skin like no woman in years.

Like no woman since Brenda, a traitorous voice whispered in his head.

But given what he was about to suggest, he knew he'd have to agree to her terms. "Okay," he agreed, "but it might be harder than you think."

Her eyes narrowed. "Why?"

"Because I don't intend to let you live alone out there by the bay while there's someone stalking you," he answered, bracing for her reaction.

Her eyes narrowed. "What are you suggesting—that I hire a bodyguard?"

That would be the obvious answer, he realized, surprised he hadn't thought of it himself. It would be a lot less messy and complicated than what he'd had in mind.

"Or you could have me for free," he blurted, as if his gut wanted to get the idea out there before his head could talk him out of it.

She stared at him, her eyes dark with wariness and something else, something glittery and hot. He felt an answering heat low in his gut, a stark reminder of how difficult the next few days would be if she agreed to what he was suggesting.

"I can take care of myself," she said, her voice faint.

"I know."

"Then why?"

"You're a cop. When you and your fellow deputies go out on dangerous calls, do you go alone?"

"No."

"Safety in numbers." He leaned toward her, his chest tight with tension. "You've seen my files. You know how those women died. You know how he got to them. For that one moment, nobody was watching their backs."

Moisture pooled in her eyes, making them shine.

"Brenda wanted me to resign from the Navy. It was never supposed to be my career, you know—I was going to serve my country a few years, save up a little money and then we'd buy us a house on the lake and raise our kids—" He stopped short, pain constricting his throat.

"Best-laid plans," she murmured.

"If I'd been there, she'd have called me. I'd have gone there and fixed her car—" He grimaced. "It was an old piece of crap anyway. I should have replaced it long before it gave out on her, but we were saving as much money as we could."

"What happened to her wasn't your fault."

"And Carrie's death wasn't yours. But you blame yourself anyway, don't you?"

She looked down at her hands. "She wanted me to meet her there, but we were crossways about Hamilton, and I just found something else to do that night. At least until I started worrying about her."

"They both needed someone watching their backs, and we didn't realize it until too late." He reached across the table, taking her hand firmly. "You need someone to watch your back. I wasn't there for Brenda. Please let me be there for you."

She knew he was right—he could see the look of resignation in her green eyes—but he also knew she took pride in being self-sufficient and strong. She didn't want to admit she needed anyone's help.

She pulled her hand away from his, and for a second, he thought she was going to refuse him. But when she spoke, she said, "I have a spare room. It's not huge, and I'll have to get it ready for habitation—"

"I can help you."

Now that she'd made the decision, she seemed to relax, even slanting an amused look his way. "Tell the truth—you're really in this for temporary joint custody of my grill."

"I do love your grill," he admitted, grinning at her.

She smiled back at him. "If you'll cook every night, this might be the best thing that ever happened to me."

They fell silent, but the tension that had thickened the air between them was mostly gone, replaced by a watchful sort of truce, one J.D. was loath to shatter by speaking. But something she'd said earlier niggled at his memory. "You said you wanted to call me when you found the file. Just to tell me about it, or was there something more specific?"

"That's right, I didn't ask you—do you know if Victor Logan could have been in the Terrebonne area twelve years ago?"

He thought about it. There was a lot about Logan's movements that remained a mystery. "I know he was working in Chickasaw County at the time of Brenda's death. We've traced him in the area as far back as six months before her murder, but he left town a couple of weeks afterward, the best we can tell. Nobody knew where he went. He didn't ask anyone for work references, but apparently that's not unheard of for people who travel from job to job the way he did."

"That's the last you know about him until he showed up in Buckley, Mississippi?"

"He spent some time in the New Orleans area, because that's where he met my sister-in-law." He'd already told Natalie about his sister-in-law Mariah's connection to Victor—how her suspicion of his possible involvement in Brenda's murder was what had led her to Gossamer Ridge in the first place, where she'd met his brother Jake and married him after a whirlwind courtship. "She shared a house with Victor for a few years before he was arrested, but she said he spent a lot of time away from home over that time and could have been involved in any number of murders within driving distance of Buckley."

"Terrebonne is within driving distance," she pointed out. "It's a two-hour drive."

"But the murder you're talking about happened several years before he got to Buckley."

"I think we're looking at this the wrong way," she said. "We're worried about where Victor Logan was living at the time when the real question is, where was the alpha killer living?"

"If we knew who he was, we'd be in a better position to figure that out."

She nodded. "I have to get back to work. But here." She pulled a key ring from her jacket pocket and removed a key from the ring. "This is my house key. Do you have something to write with? I need to give you the alarm code."

He had a pen in his shirt pocket. He gave it to her and pushed a clean napkin toward her. "Just write it down. Don't want anyone to overhear it."

She grabbed the napkin and wrote the code on it, glancing around to make sure no one was looking. She handed the pen and the napkin back to him. "Let yourself in. I'll call if I'm going to be any later than six-thirty. Raid my freezer and see what you're in the mood to grill." She flashed him an unexpected smile that lit up the whole diner. "Surprise me."

After they paid for lunch, she walked him to his truck, pausing by his door while he unlocked it. "J.D., this has to be strictly business. You know that, right?"

He turned to look at her, disarmed by the wariness in her eyes. "I know we should keep it that way, yes."

"We *will* keep it that way," she said firmly. "I can't do casual relationships. Hell, I can't do relationships, period, apparently. So if you're looking for someone who'll be okay with a temporary shackup—"

"That's not what I'm looking for," he protested. "I'm not looking for anything."

"Which amounts to the same thing. And I'm just not up for that, okay?"

He started to reach out and touch her arm, to try to reassure her that his intentions were nothing but honorable, but he knew that was only part of the truth. Hell, his whole body seemed to be humming with fire just because she was standing close enough to touch. His intentions might be honorable, but his desires were anything but. Maybe her wariness was warranted. He dropped his hand to his side.

He couldn't let his baser urges get in his way. She was clearly in danger, and he could help her. And maybe together, they could find the answers about his wife's murder that had eluded him all these years.

"Okay, he said aloud. He'd just have to find some way to keep his hands to himself, and not just for her sake.

God knew, he didn't want any more regrets in his own life, either.

Natalie felt a flutter of reckless anticipation when she spotted J.D.'s truck parked under the tall stilts supporting her house that evening. She pulled the Lexus into the space next to his and walked under the house to the steps leading up to the back balcony.

The smoky aroma of grilling meat lured her up the steps, where she found J.D. working at the grill, flipping jumbo Gulf shrimp with a pair of tongs. He looked up at her approach, his blue eyes smoldering. An answering flutter low in her belly made her stop at a safe distance.

"Shrimp's a good choice," she said. "I approve."

"I stopped at the fish market. I bought some salad stuff, too—your refrigerator contents would make my poor mother cry."

She chuckled. "Let's don't tell her, then. I'll go start on the salad."

He caught her arm as she began to pass him, heading for the door into the house. Instantly, her body turned into one raw nerve ending set aflame by the touch. She met his gaze, her breath hitching.

He stared back, his eyes dilating until only a thin rim of blue remained. Suddenly, he dragged his gaze away and cleared his throat. "Um, first take a look at that paper on the table over there." He gestured toward the small round patio table, where a large piece of legal paper lay, anchored in place against the light breeze off the bay by a citronella candle holder.

When she drew closer, she saw that J.D. had drawn a crude map of the Gulf states—Louisiana, Mississippi and Alabama. He'd drawn dots on the map, each dot with a name beside it. Adele Phillips in Saraland. Vivian Nettles in Meridian. Two coeds killed in Millbridge three hours north of Terrebonne. Other murders scattered across southern Mississippi and Alabama. Two murders in the New Orleans area.

And one in Gossamer Ridge, Alabama.

"Why Gossamer Ridge?" she asked aloud. She looked over at J.D., who stood by the grill, nodding at her.

"That's what struck me. All the other murders are along the Gulf coast area. Brenda's is the outlier—Gossamer Ridge is almost six hours from the coast."

"It's not just that," she said, looking back at the hand-drawn map. "All of the murders happened in areas within a three-hour drive from Terrebonne." She picked up the pen he'd been using and, using Terrebonne as her starting point, she drew lines to each of the murder sites. The lines spread out from the small bay town like rays of the sun.

"Terrebonne," she said aloud.

"Terrebonne," he agreed. "And I think that may explain why Gossamer Ridge, too."

"Because Brenda was from here."

He nodded again. "I think Brenda was the first murder, and I think he sought her out on purpose. Because he knew her personally." His gaze captured hers, afire with an old, white-hot fury. "The son of a bitch lives right here in Terrebonne."

Chapter Thirteen

"It could be Terrebonne, or just Ridley County," J.D. said later, as they shared a plate of grilled shrimp and vegetables over the map he'd drawn.

Natalie swatted away a mosquito. "Ten thousand people in the county, five thousand here in Terrebonne." Grabbing the box of matches on the table, she lit the citronella candle. The scent wafting from its flickering flame reminded J.D. of lazy family cookouts on the back deck of his parents' lake house. He wished the rest of the Coopers were here with him right now. The more time he spent alone with Natalie, the less certain he became that staying here tonight was a good idea.

It had been a long time since he'd wanted a woman as badly as he wanted Natalie right now.

But why? Why her? She was a pretty woman, certainly, but he knew plenty of women more beautiful. More shapely, more glamorous, more openly sexual and seductive.

Right now, she looked tired, her clothes rumpled from a long day at the sheriff's station and her hair escaping in messy tendrils from the ponytail at the base of her neck. Her makeup had worn off during the day, save for a smoky smudge of smeared mascara beneath each green eye. Her tailored blouse looked almost masculine and shapeless, and the Smith & Wesson riding in a chunky holster at her hip was nearly as big as his SIG.

He ought to have no trouble keeping his mind on the case they were trying to crack—the case he'd been trying to crack for more than a decade. The man they were looking for killed Brenda. Why wasn't that enough to keep him focused tonight?

"J.D.?" Natalie's voice penetrated his mental haze.

He met her questioning gaze. "Yes?"

"I asked if Brenda ever mentioned having a stalker."

The question caught him by surprise. "Not that I remember. I think she'd have told me or at least my parents if someone in Gossamer Ridge was giving her a hard time."

"I meant here in Terrebonne."

"Oh." Brenda had never mentioned having trouble with anyone when she was still living at home, though he did remember being surprised when she wanted to move to Gossamer Ridge to live while he was doing his overseas duty.

"What is it?" Natalie asked, apparently reading his expression. "Did you remember something?"

"When Brenda and I first married, I was about to go on a two-year overseas stint. I figured she'd just stay here with her folks, since it was close to the Naval Station in Pensacola. But she insisted on moving to Gossamer Ridge. I had a house there already, but it wasn't really habitable, since I was never there. She said she wanted something that was just ours. I just figured she wanted to start our married life even if it was without me for a little while."

"Now you're not so sure?"

"What if she was looking for an excuse to get out of Terrebonne? She didn't visit here much—her parents visited up there most of the time. All the time, once the kids were born. Brenda wasn't a selfish person, so I figured that's just what they decided to do between them." He rubbed the back of his neck. "I assumed they liked getting away from the coast now and then. Gossamer Ridge is beautiful—it's not a hardship to visit there."

"If she had a stalker here, she'd want to get away," Natalie said. "Up there, she'd be surrounded by your family, far away from whoever was bothering her."

"But why wouldn't she tell me about it?"

"I don't know. You could ask her parents."

He remembered his vague promise to his mother-in-law that he'd be by to visit soon. "I could drop by tomorrow. George will probably be at the office, but Lois should be around."

Natalie reached across the table, closing her slim fingers over his hand. Even the light touch sent fire pouring through his veins until his whole body seemed to burn.

Her eyes darkened, reflecting whatever it was she saw in his gaze. She pulled her hand away, leaving him feeling bereft. She cleared her throat and looked away. "It could be a coincidence—even if someone was stalking her."

"Maybe," he conceded. "But what if she was his first murder? What if he went to Gossamer Ridge to stalk her and kill her?"

"How does Victor Logan figure in, then?" Natalie gathered the remains of their dinner, her movements restless.

J.D. followed her into the kitchen. "I'm not sure. It could be that the alpha killer met Logan in Gossamer Ridge. Maybe he needed someone to help him get to Brenda without making her suspicious. We know Victor Logan was doing work for the trucking company. He could have paid Victor to get him into the building."

"And Victor liked the vicarious thrill of murder so much he offered to keep being his front man for free?" Natalie turned at the counter, her eyes widening at how close he stood. Her tongue darted out to wet her lips, stoking the fire in his belly.

"Maybe that's exactly what happened." He should move

away from her, give her space to slip out between him and the counter, but he couldn't convince his legs to work. He could only stand there, gazing down into her wide green eyes and struggling to focus on what they were talking about.

She leaned against the counter, her fingers clutching the edges until her knuckles whitened. "Isn't that how it works?" Her voice was raspy and low. "The beta killer acts as his front man. He's probably someone nobody would suspect—"

"Like a mechanic or a grad student," J.D. agreed, thrusting his hands into the pockets of his jeans to keep from touching her.

"I wonder who he's using here."

"If these murders are even connected," J.D. reminded her. "You've never been sure Carrie's murder was connected, and the Moss Crossing murder is problematic—"

"But if the beta killer committed the Moss Crossing murder, it could explain the differences in the M.O.," she pointed out. Her chin lifted with determination, but it was no match for the vulnerability in her eyes. "And maybe I'm wrong about Carrie's murder. It does fit the profile of the other murders."

His hands came free of his pockets before he could stop himself, and he cradled her face between his hands. "I'm going to find out. It's got to end here."

She leaned toward him until her forehead came to a rest against his chin. "I don't know how you've survived all these years without knowing who killed your wife. It hasn't even been a month since Carrie's death, and I can't find a moment's peace."

She never would, he knew. Not until her sister's murderer—or murderers—saw justice.

For a moment, he was content to simply stand there, his hands resting lightly on her shoulders while she leaned into his body. There was something comforting about the closeness that lulled him into believing perhaps they could make it through the night without succumbing to temptation after all.

And then her hands lifted to his waist, her fingers moving with slow determination against his rib cage. He drew his head back and found her gazing up at him with fire in her eyes, and he knew they didn't have a chance in hell of getting out of this whole mess unscathed.

She brushed her lips against the side of his neck, and he couldn't swallow a groan of need. "Natalie, I don't think this is strictly businesslike—"

Her answer was to nip at the tendon at the base of his neck. He shuddered, struggling against the urge to lift her onto the kitchen counter and take her right there. He tried to curb his impulses, since Natalie seemed to have no intention of keeping him in check, but each touch of her mouth to his throat, his chest, the curve of his chin was like a hammer blow, chipping away at his control until it crumbled around his feet.

He wrapped his arms around her waist and lifted her onto the counter, inflamed by her low, feral growl. She pulled him to her, parting her thighs to welcome him between them. He couldn't stop his hips from thrusting against the softness he found there, especially when that guttural noise escaped her throat again.

She threaded her fingers in his hair and drew his face up, slanting her mouth over his with fierce hunger. Her tongue slid over his, hot and sweet, moving with a ferocious determination that he was powerless to resist. He'd never felt so out of control before, not even with Brenda, who had been a joyous, generous lover.

Brenda, he thought.

It was only when Natalie went utterly still that he realized he'd said the name aloud.

She dropped her hands to her side slowly, staring at him with eyes as dark and pained as a bruise.

"Natalie—"

She wriggled off the counter and darted away. He turned to find her standing at the back window, staring at the bay.

"Look—you don't know what that meant—"

"I'm really tired now, J.D. Long days at work. Don't worry about the dishes. I'll clean up tomorrow morning—" She headed toward the hallway that led to the bedrooms.

He followed her to her door, not out of any conscious thought but because his legs seemed incapable of doing anything else. She whirled around to face him, her expression implacable.

"Don't do this, J.D."

"I didn't mistake you for my wife."

"Your late wife."

He flinched.

"Exactly." She caught his left hand in hers, running her thumb over the gold band he still wore. "You're not ready to let go. And that's okay. I just can't get in the middle of that."

"I know she's not coming back," he said, even as he had to acknowledge what she was saying. He wasn't ready to give Brenda up. He wouldn't be until he found out who killed her. Nor could he know for sure, until the time came, that he'd be able to let her go once he finally found the truth.

She let go of his hand. "Let's just forget that happened, okay? Chalk it up to hormones or whatever you want to call it. I can't do this. I could lie to myself and pretend there's some hope that what happened here tonight would be more that just sex, but we both know it wouldn't be."

He wasn't sure that was true, but he had no grounds to argue with her. She deserved more than he could give her.

He retreated until his back pressed against the wall behind him. "I'm sorry."

"No need. I started it. I ended it. No harm done." She turned and disappeared into her room, leaving him alone in the silent hallway.

No harm done, he silently echoed.

He definitely knew that wasn't true.

NATALIE HAD HOPED TO leave the house before J.D. awoke, but he came into the kitchen while she was polishing off a cup of yogurt. He had donned jeans and a T-shirt—his usual choice of attire—but his feet were bare and his short-cropped hair was mussed, as if he'd just rolled out of bed.

She averted her eyes before her imagination took her back down the sultry path it had taken for most of the night, depriving her of all but a couple hours of restless sleep.

How had she let herself get so entangled with a man like J. D. Cooper, a man who still wore his wedding ring twelve years after his wife's death? A man who couldn't kiss her without calling his dead wife's name? It wasn't as if she hadn't seen trouble coming from a mile away. She'd known the second she turned to see him standing in that cemetery that he was dangerous, and nothing that had happened between them since had done anything to change her mind. So why had she been stupid enough to let herself get so caught up in his drama?

"Headed into the station so early?

"I've got to finish up some paperwork, so I thought I'd get an early start."

"If you're doing it to avoid me, forget it. I'm going to go see if I can get my room at the motel back." He scrubbed his hand over the top of his head, smoothing down his spiky bedhead. "But I don't think you should stay here alone. Maybe you should go back to your parents' place for a while."

The very thought of slinking back home to her parents again made her skin crawl. "I'll figure out something."

He took a step toward her. Even though he didn't make a move to touch her, she'd swear she could feel the heat of his body, as real as a touch, as it snaked around her, drawing her in. "I mean it, Natalie. You can't stay here by yourself with someone sending you threats."

She struggled against her body's insistent urge to close the distance remaining between them. "It was just flowers."

"And someone trying to gun you down in the motel parking lot," he reminded her.

She made herself look at him. "I'll work it out."

"What does that mean?"

"It means I'm not something you have to worry about. I absolve you of all responsibility."

"You can't absolve me."

"Why not?"

"Because it won't make me feel any less guilty if something happens to you." His voice lowered a notch. "If something happens to you—"

She closed her eyes, unable to bear the real pain she saw burning in his gaze. "I'll go to my parents' house," she said, although she wasn't sure she'd keep that promise. She'd used the excuse of the party planning to explain her return home to the family mansion the night before the fundraiser, but she didn't have that excuse available now.

Her father had been waiting for years for her to crawl home and admit she'd made a mistake taking the job with the sheriff's department. He'd just love it if she had to admit she wasn't capable of protecting herself without his help.

"I've got to go see the Teagues this morning. I talked to Lois last night before I went to bed. Mike spent the night with his cousins again, so they'll both be there alone if I go early enough. I'll come back and get my things when I'm done there, and drop off the key at the station." He dipped his head, forcing her to look at him again. "Promise me you'll either find a place to stay or you'll get someone you trust to stay here with you."

She sighed. "I promise." Even if she decided against going to her parents' house, maybe she could ask Travis to stay here at her place for a few days. He didn't have any romantic designs on her, and he'd probably enjoy the novelty of playing bodyguard. He'd been complaining about the boredom of his patrol duty.

"Good."

She threw away the half-eaten cup of yogurt and grabbed her purse from the counter. She had a toothbrush in her locker at the station, it would save her from having to stick around here to say goodbye.

Cut it off fast and clean. Best way to get through it was to get it over with.

"I may not be around when you drop off the key—I'm probably going to do some searching through the cold case archives in the annex. Just leave the key in my desk."

He frowned. "I'd rather give it directly to you—I don't want to give anyone a chance to sneak it out and make a copy."

He was right, she knew, but it irritated her anyway. She didn't want to have to see him again after she walked out the door. "Fine. If I'm not back, you can wait until I get back." She headed for the door.

When he followed her, well-bred politeness forced her to turn and bid him goodbye.

"Why does this have to be the end of everything?" he asked. "I mean, I get that you don't want things to get complicated, and I get why it's a bad idea to stay here, but I can still help you find the man who killed your sister and maybe my wife."

"I don't think there's any way to work together without things getting complicated, J.D. And I just can't deal with that. Let's just end it now. Quick and clean." The hurt in his eyes delivered a swift punch to her resolve, but she stood her ground. "Let me know if you have any trouble getting another room. I can pull some strings."

She turned and headed for her car, steeling herself to keep from turning back for one last look.

Chapter Fourteen

"You look tired." Lois Teague poured J.D. a cup of coffee in her sunny kitchen and set it on the table in front of him.

"Didn't sleep well." He smiled his thanks as Lois brought her own cup of coffee to the table and sat across from him.

"Are you seeing Natalie Becker?"

J.D. choked on his coffee, the scalding liquid burning his throat. Lois calmly handed him a napkin. "Did Mike say something?" he asked in a strangled voice.

Lois shot him a wry smile. "I believe his exact words were, 'Dad was macking on some woman.'"

J.D. sighed. "I've raised him well."

"You have, you know. He's a good boy."

"Credit for that belongs to my parents."

"You've had more influence on him than you may think." Lois reached across the table, laying her slender hand on J.D.'s arm. "And if you *are* seeing Natalie Becker, it's okay with George and me. We never expected you to bury yourself with our daughter."

He winced at her words, wishing he could protest that he hadn't been doing any such thing. But she knew better.

Lois patted his arm. "Besides, I like Natalie. She's a lonely soul, and maybe a little hard to get to know, but she treats people with kindness, folks her family doesn't normally notice. Brenda would have liked her."

He felt an odd sense of pride in her words, somehow gladdened by the fact that Lois could see the same things in Natalie that had drawn him to her in the first place. "She's good people," he agreed. "But we're not a couple."

"I'm sorry to hear that. I'd like to see you happy again."

He squeezed her hand, both grateful for her support and burning with rage that their daughter's death had stolen all the years of happiness that had once spread before them like jewels. "Thank you, Lois."

"But I don't think you came here to talk about your love life," Lois said after a brief but oddly comfortable silence. "You're here because of Brenda's murder, aren't you?"

He nodded. "There are a few things I haven't told you yet."

Her eyes darkened. "About Victor Logan?"

He nodded. "We have good reason to believe he wasn't acting alone. In fact, we're pretty sure that Victor was only an accessory to Brenda's murder in the first place."

Lois put one hand over her mouth, pain glittering in her eyes. "You mean—"

"If Logan didn't kill Brenda, who did?"

The sound of George Teague's voice behind him made J.D.'s whole body jerk with surprise. He must have come in the front of the house without their hearing the door. "Hello, George."

Brenda's father pulled out the chair next to J.D. and leaned forward, his gaze burning with fierce intensity. "Why didn't you tell us about this?"

"I only found out about it a few weeks ago." J.D. outlined Alicia's theory of the serial killer pair and explained the connection between Victor Logan, Marlon Dyson and the mystery man they knew only as Alex. "We think Alex may have found another partner and started killing again."

"Where?" Lois asked.

"Right here," George answered before J.D. could. "Carrie

Becker. I was called to the restaurant that night—the county M.E. was out of town on a conference. I declared her dead."

"Then you saw the way the body was positioned," J.D. murmured, regret raw in his voice. George knew enough about his daughter's murder to have seen the similarities. What must he have been thinking all this time? Had he suspected?

"I knew it looked the same. But Victor Logan was dead—so I told myself it couldn't be connected." George laid his head in his hands. "So the bastard's killing down here now?"

"I think he's from here," J.D. answered. "I think Brenda was his first murder, and he went up there specifically to kill her. Then I guess, once he had a taste of it, he just kept doing it. So he could get that feeling again and again."

George's gaze whipped up. "Carrie looked a lot like Brenda. It would catch me by surprise, sometimes, if I ran into her on the street." He rubbed his clean-shaven jaw. "This monster's been killing our girl over and over, all these years?"

"Why did she move to Gossamer Ridge instead of staying down here when I went overseas?" J.D. asked.

George and Lois exchanged a quick look.

"What is it?" J.D. pressed. "Was someone bothering her?"

George met his gaze, cold rage crackling in his eyes. "Oh, yeah. There was."

"Who?"

George's lips thinned to an angry line. "Hamilton Gray."

"THAT PLACE IS CREEPY." Mike Cooper's cousin Derek pulled his bike up behind Mike, peering over his shoulder at the slumbering facade of Annabelle's.

Mike glanced at the younger boy, wishing he'd left him back at his Uncle Clay's house. Derek was only eleven, and small for his age. Plus, he had an annoying tendency to cry like a baby whenever something freaked him out, like a snake crawling in the woods ahead of him or, in this case, a spooky old restaurant.

But the only way Derek would agree to let Mike borrow his new ten-speed was if Mike let him tag along. Derek had borrowed his sister's, Lizzie's, bike. It wouldn't be a bad ride if it weren't a girl's bike. But it *was* a girl's bike, and Derek looked like a dork riding it.

"It's just a building," Mike said, trying not to let too much of his scorn show. It wasn't really Derek's fault that he was a wuss, the way Aunt Judy babied him all the time. And even though he knew where Mike wanted to go, Derek had refused to stay behind. Sure, he'd tried to talk Mike out of going, and he'd whined about their destination the whole trip here, but at least he didn't chicken out. The kid had potential.

"I'm going home," Derek said, his voice lowering to a frantic hiss. "Some woman got killed here. Just a few weeks ago. What if the guy who killed her is in there right now?"

"He's not in there right now," Mike scoffed, although there was a part of him that wondered if Derek could be right. Didn't killers always come back to the scene of the crime?

As far as he knew, nobody had ever come back to the scene of his mother's murder. He'd gone there once, with Cissy, his sister. It was only three years ago, after she got her license. He'd overheard her tell her friend Anna that she was going to drive to the old abandoned warehouse where Belmont Trucking had once had its headquarters, and he'd blackmailed her into taking him with her.

She remembered their mom. He didn't, really, that was why it was hard to feel anything but bewilderment, standing on a winter-bare patch of ground where his Uncle Gabe had found his mother's body. Cissy had cried a little that day, but Mike had only felt a vague, queasy sort of twisting in his gut, as if something dark and cold had crept up his spine to settle in his chest.

"I want to go home, Mike. Come on!"

"You can go, but I'm staying."

"Trade bikes."

"No way." Mike wouldn't be caught dead on a girl's bike. He headed for the restaurant, forcing Derek to make a choice.

Mike heard the sound of his cousin's bike speeding away. He looked over his shoulder and saw that Derek was already halfway to the bend where the road wound through the woods. Uncle Clay's house was only a couple of miles in that direction, an easy ride, even on a girl's ten-speed. Derek would be okay.

Meanwhile, Mike wanted to know just what it was that had fascinated his father and that cop lady enough to take them inside the abandoned restaurant. If his dad didn't want to fill him in on the details, he'd just have to find out for himself.

"HAMILTON GRAY?" J.D. stared at his father-in-law. "As in Carrie Gray's husband?"

George Teague nodded. "He was crazy about Brenda when he was younger. A lot of boys liked her, and I suppose she liked them well enough, too, but she never cared for Hamilton at all. Said he gave her a creepy feeling, always staring at her and trying to sit with her at lunch at school. He was a couple of years older than she was, and you know she was such a sensible girl—"

"A lot of girls would've jumped at the chance to date Hamilton," Lois added. "He was a handsome boy, and rich as Croesus. Girls always enjoyed the attention of a senior—"

"What was a rich kid like Gray doing going to public high school?" J.D. asked.

"I believe that was when his father was running for governor, wasn't it, George?" Lois looked over at her husband, who nodded.

"Old Milton Gray thought he'd have a better chance looking like a man of the people if his kids weren't attending a private

prep-school in Mobile, so he enrolled them in public school."
George looked at J.D. "It didn't stop after he graduated. He
deferred college for a few years, supposedly to work on his
father's later senate campaign—"

"Also a failure," Lois said with a hint of satisfaction that
caught J.D. by surprise. Lois was about the least vindictive
person he knew, so for her to take pleasure in someone else's
misfortune was notable. "But it kept Hamilton in Terrebonne
for two more years. We thought things would finally get better
when he went off to Harvard—"

"But he came home on holidays and summers," George
finished for her. "Made Brenda absolutely miserable."

"And nobody tried to stop him?" J.D. asked, anger roiling
in his chest like lava.

"Oh, we tried. But the Grays are influential, wealthy
people. And Hamilton was subtle about it. What could the
police do, arrest him every time he showed up somewhere
Brenda was?"

"Has he ever been one to get in trouble? Maybe playing
with matches or killing stray dogs—"

"You know, there was that spate of dog killings about
twenty-five years ago," Lois said to George. "Remember, the
Lawson's little Yorkie disappeared just down the street—
found later in the street, torn apart, poor thing."

"Animal control figured a coyote or maybe a big owl had
gotten him, but they weren't looking hard," George said. "I
heard of at least a dozen other pets disappearing around that
time."

"How old would Hamilton Gray have been?"

"Maybe sixteen?" Lois answered. "Brenda was fourteen, I
think—still riding a bike to school instead of driving. She's the
one who found the little Yorkie, right outside our house."

J.D. grimaced.

George's brow creased. "You think he killed the dog

and put him in front of our house for Brenda to find, don't you?"

"Was he interested in her that far back?"

"We suspected so," Lois answered. "They were a good family, and we wouldn't have objected at first, but Brenda had better sense than her folks."

J.D. pushed to his feet. "I've got to go. There's something I need to look into—"

George stood with him. "You're not going after Hamilton Gray. You'd never get anywhere near him."

"We'll see," J.D. said with a grim smile. "But not yet."

First, he needed to track down Natalie and tell her the latest information. If what he was thinking was true, maybe they were both right about who killed her sister, Carrie, after all.

NATALIE'S CELL PHONE vibrated on her desk. J. D. Cooper's number again. She hit the ignore button and continued filing.

At his desk nearby, Massey glanced her way. "Creditors?" he asked wryly. "Oh, wait, sorry. Beckers don't do debt, do they?"

Natalie flashed him a crude gesture that made him laugh.

"If it's not the credit bureau, must be a guy." Massey craned his neck as if trying to see the display window on her phone. "Let me guess—tall, dark and widower calling?"

She ignored the bait. "Wrong number."

The phone buzzed again. She jabbed the ignore button with a little more force.

"I know you're rich enough to buy yourself a dozen new phones, but think about the environment, Becker. Trash that phone and it'll spend decades in a landfill—"

She slammed the file drawer shut and glared at him. "You know, I thought we were getting along better these days, Massey, but right now you're all over my nerves."

He held up his hands in defense. "Chill, Becker. It means you're one of the guys. I thought you wanted that."

She softened her features. "You're right. I do. And I appreciate the fact that you're not treating me like I'm a rattlesnake in your sleeping bag anymore. But did you have to go straight from that to bratty little brother?"

"I do have years of practice. Ask my sister, Dana."

"I'll look her up and find out how to make you stop." Her cell phone buzzed again. She shoved it in her pocket. "I think I'm going to take an early lunch. Want anything while I'm out?"

"No, I'm meeting a friend for lunch later."

Natalie shot him a look. "Does Massey have a girl-friend?"

"Becker?" a voice interrupted.

Natalie looked up to see Travis Rayburn standing in the bullpen doorway. "Yeah?"

"Your father just left a message at the front desk." He handed her a slip of paper from a message pad.

Natalie read the message. *Father called—meet at Annabelle's at eleven-thirty.* She glanced at her watch. Eleven-fifteen. "Did he say what it was about?"

Travis shook his head. "Daniels took the call, and he didn't say. I just offered to pass along the message."

Maybe he'd found someone interested in buying the place, she thought. She grabbed her jacket and shrugged it on, turning to Massey. "I'm taking an early lunch. My father wants to see me. Be back in about an hour."

She looked for Daniels at the front desk to see if her father had given him any more details, but another deputy manned the desk, ear to the phone as he took down information from someone on the other end of the line. Daniels must be at lunch.

In her car, she tried her father's cell phone. It went straight to voicemail. He was probably on the phone.

As she started to put the phone down, she saw the handful of missed calls from J. D. Cooper. Should she call him back? What if he had new information about the case.

With a sigh, she checked to see if he'd left her a voicemail. He had, on the last try. "Natalie, I need to see you. Call me when you get this."

Her finger hovered over the dial-back option, but she shut off the phone and stuck it back in her pocket. First, she'd see what her father wanted with her.

She could always call J.D. later.

NOW THAT HIS COUSIN Derek was well out of sight, Mike Cooper began to second-guess his decision to find a way inside the abandoned restaurant. He could practically hear his Uncle Aaron's voice in his head, quoting Alabama laws on breaking and entering.

Not that he was going to steal anything—he was no thief. In fact, he planned to join the Chickasaw County Sheriff's Department as soon as he was old enough.

He suddenly found himself missing his sister, Cissy, much to his surprise. Most of the time, she was a big, bossy pest. He supposed it was because she saw herself as a substitute mom, even though she wasn't that much older than he was—just six and a half years. That was hardly anything at all.

But Cissy was smart. And she was good at stuff like this— she'd know how to get into the restaurant and not leave any trace that she had been there. She was going to be an FBI agent, or at least, that was her latest ambition.

Mike had a sneaking suspicion she'd make it, too.

He dismounted his bike, hiding it behind the thicket of holly bushes planted at the back of the restaurant, the prickly leaves scratching his arms without drawing blood. Rubbing the scraped skin, he looked around to make sure nobody was watching before he scooted across the scrubby lot behind the restaurant to the screened-in back door.

Using the hem of his T-shirt to protect the handle from his fingerprints, Mike pulled open the screen door—which made an alarmingly loud screech. With a wince, he darted a quick look around again. No sign of anyone watching.

Still using the T-shirt, he tried the back door knob. It rattled uselessly in his hand—locked.

He stepped back and eased the screen door back into position. Sneaking into an abandoned building was one thing—picking a lock was a whole other thing. It so happened that he knew a little about lock-picking—something else Cissy had taught him—but she'd pretty much pounded into his brain the importance of using the skill only in times of dire emergency.

"You need to know how to do things," she'd told him as they practiced on the back door of their dad's house just a few weeks ago, "but you also need to know when to do them."

Slapping a mosquito nibbling at the back of his neck, he felt a twinge of guilt. Was this really a need-to situation?

Yes. The man who killed his mother before he was even old enough to walk had killed another woman right here, just a few weeks ago. He couldn't walk away from here without trying a little harder to get inside and see the crime scene for himself.

Picking the lock on the door wasn't really feasible—he didn't have any of the tools Cissy had showed him how to use. But that didn't mean there wasn't another way in.

There were six windows lining the back of the restaurant. Four of them were a little too high to be good bets, but the two flanking the back door were low enough to enable him to drag himself up and over the sill if he could get the windows open.

He checked the window on the left. The lock was engaged, so he scooted over to the other window and checked the lock. A flutter of excitement darted through his belly. It was unlocked.

Pulling his penknife from the pocket of his jeans, Mike pried the screen away from the window. With a little jiggling, he was able to pop open the latches and remove the screen, laying it on the ground propped against the wall of the restaurant.

Mike pushed the window upward. It creaked and groaned, old paint cracking under the force, but it finally gave, inching up. With a low grunt, he pushed the window up further, creating an opening about eighteen inches high. He squeezed through the gap and landed with an awkward thud on the floor of the restaurant kitchen.

He started to push to his feet when he realized he was looking straight at a pair of brown-leather shoes.

His heart skipping a beat, he stared at the tall, sandy-haired man gazing at him. "What are you doing here?" he blurted.

The man's lips curved into a faint smile. "You're her son, aren't you? You look just like her."

An ache settled low in Mike's gut as he pushed to his feet, wishing he hadn't pocketed his pen knife. Because the man standing in front of him was holding a gun.

"I'm Hamilton Gray," the man said. "I knew your mother well. Very well indeed."

Chapter Fifteen

"Damn it!" J.D. shoved the phone in his pocket, refusing to leave another voicemail as he pulled into the parking lot of the Ridley County Sheriff's Department. Clearly, Natalie didn't want to talk to him on the phone.

Too bad. He had to talk to her. Now.

He left his SIG in the truck, locked safely in its case, knowing from his last, unwilling visit here that visitors had to go through a metal detector to enter the building. He made it through the check without incident and asked for Natalie Becker at the front desk. The deputy sent him down the hall into what was apparently the deputies' communal office.

He spotted Massey at one of the desks, but Natalie wasn't there. He made his way through the room to Massey's desk.

Massey's eyebrows quirked. "Mr. Cooper. Please don't tell me you've been picked up for trespassing again."

"I'm looking for Natalie," J.D. answered. "Is she here?"

"No, she got a call from her father and headed out for an early lunch."

J.D. frowned. Based on what little Natalie had told him about her strained relationship with her father, a sudden lunch invitation seemed odd. "Are you sure she was meeting her father?"

"That's what she said."

"Did he call her directly?"

"No, she got a message." Massey frowned. "That's odd, isn't it? Why wouldn't he call her cell phone?"

"Who gave her the message?"

"Rayburn, but he got it from Daniels at the front desk."

"Thanks." J.D. headed back to the front of the sheriff's station, where the deputy who'd directed him to the bullpen sat talking to a pretty blond file clerk.

"Are you Daniels?" J.D. interrupted.

The deputy shot him an irritated look. "Who's asking?"

Tamping down his frustration, J.D. told the man his name. "I'm trying to find Natalie Becker. You took a call for her from her father earlier—did he say what he wanted with her?"

Daniels frowned. "I didn't take any calls for Becker today, and especially not from her father."

J.D.'s gut tightened. "Are you sure?"

"Yeah, I think I'd remember talking to one of the richest guys in the state."

"That's odd." Doyle Massey's voice made J.D. turn. Massey stood nearby, looking worried. "Rayburn definitely said Daniels took the call."

"I can check the phone logs," Daniels suggested.

"Do that," J.D. said. He pulled out his phone and dialed Natalie's number again. It went directly to voicemail. He shut it off with a growl.

"No calls came for Becker," Daniels said.

J.D.'s gut tightened as a new flurry of fear settled into the pit of his gut. Was he letting his imagination get the best of him? Fathers and daughters met for lunch all the time.

But given the information he'd learned from the Teagues today, he didn't dare ignore his gut feeling of dread.

He turned to Massey. "Where's Rayburn?"

ANNABELLE'S LOOMED OUT of nowhere as Natalie rounded the curve on Sedge Road, the low-slung facade a bittersweet reminder, as always, of her sister. Carrie had held such high hopes for the place. Perhaps a little too high—her father had taken a certain paternal pleasure in reminding his younger daughter of the perils of the restaurant business.

"Most restaurants fail," Natalie murmured aloud in the silence of her car.

Mine will succeed, Carrie had insisted. Natalie suspected her sister would have been right. Just about everything Carrie touched turned to gold.

Everything but her marriage.

She pulled into the parking lot, surprised that her father's Mercedes sedan wasn't waiting there for her already. She parked in front and checked her phone to see if her father had called to say he'd be late. She'd shut the phone off to avoid seeing J.D.'s name on her phone display, but she hadn't considered that she'd also miss calls from her father.

It didn't matter. No calls from her father. She called and left him a message that she was at Annabelle's and could wait only a little while longer.

She also noted that J.D. had called twice since she shut off the phone. His sheer doggedness was beginning to worry her. What did he want? Had something happened she needed to know about?"

With a sigh, she tried his number. It went straight to voicemail. "Damn it." She left a quick message. "It's Natalie. I'm meeting my father but I'll call back later." She shut the phone back off and put it in her purse.

Leaning back against the seat, she wondered what her father wanted. She shouldn't be surprised he was late; for all his talk about punctuality, he watched the clock only when it pertained to work. Family could always wait.

He was probably stuck in a meeting. Or ran by a store to meet with a vendor. Anything work-related could have held him up.

She stared through the windshield at the restaurant facade,

remembering the last time she was here, with J.D. That had been a disaster, hadn't it? She was getting very good at creating disasters. Too bad she wasn't getting any better at warding them off before they arrived.

The interior of the Lexus was beginning to get hot. Prickles of sweat bloomed on her skin, a rivulet of perspiration sliding down her back between her shoulder blades, but she couldn't bring herself to go into the restaurant. She knew she would smell the phantom blood again. She would picture the scene of her sister's murder in haunting detail.

Why had her father wanted to meet her here of all places?

J.D. TRIED NATALIE AGAIN while waiting in the deputies' bullpen for Travis Rayburn to show up. No answer, but when he hung up the call, he saw a message waiting from her, telling him she was meeting her father. He tried calling her immediately, but she'd apparently turned off the phone again.

"I just got off the phone with her father," Massey said. "He's in Mobile for the day and didn't call."

J.D. spat out a profanity. "Has she tried to call him?"

"He just got out of a meeting and hasn't checked his messages on his cell yet. He said he'd call back if he found one." Massey's gaze shifted toward the doorway. "There's Rayburn."

J.D. looked up to see a wiry deputy in his mid-twenties, with short-cropped brown hair and watchful gray eyes. He gave J.D. a curious look before crossing to Massey's desk. "Daniels said you were looking for me?"

"Sit down." Massey indicated the chair by his desk.

Rayburn's eyes narrowed. "What's up?"

"Why did you tell Becker that Daniels gave you a message for her?" Massey asked.

"Because he did."

"That's not what Daniels says. And there's no call to Becker logged for today."

Rayburn glanced at J.D. "I can only tell you what Daniels told me."

"Have you ever heard of a place called Buckley, Mississippi?" J.D. asked.

Rayburn's gaze flickered his way. "Sure. It's near Hattiesburg, right?"

"Three women were murdered near Buckley over a five-year period. Are you familiar with Millbridge, Alabama?"

Rayburn's eyes narrowed. "Who *are* you?"

"This is J. D. Cooper," Massey answered.

J.D. watched him closely. There. A little flicker of recognition. Rayburn knew who he was. He knew why J.D. was there in Terrebonne.

Rage flooded J.D.'s body as all the pieces clicked into place. He stared at Rayburn, trying to see some evidence within the deputy's smoothly handsome face to prove the theory.

But the deputy's expression had gone neutral again. He actually managed a polite smile as he nodded to J.D. "Nice to meet you, Mr. Cooper."

"Cooper's investigating a string of serial murders." Massey's voice was diamond hard. "He thinks the two murders that happened around here in the last couple of months may be connected to the other murders."

"Are you a cop?" Rayburn asked genially.

"You killed the girl in Moss Crossing," J.D. said bluntly. "It's why the murder scene doesn't match—he sent you to kill for him. To set up his alibi."

Both Rayburn and Massey looked at J.D. as if he'd lost his mind. "What are you talking about?" Rayburn asked. J.D. could see Massey wanted to know the same thing. He didn't get it yet.

But he would.

"We couldn't figure out why the M.O. didn't match, even though everything else did," J.D. said to Massey.

Massey nodded, the first flicker of understanding coming into his dark eyes. "We thought it might be a copycat."

"It was." J.D. leveled his gaze with Rayburn. "You knew what to do, but when Lydia Randolph fought back, you couldn't stick to the script. That was her name, you know. Lydia Randolph. I assume you know her name, since you're the new forward scout."

Rayburn turned to look at Massey. "Is this some kind of joke, Doyle? You're just letting crazy people come in here now and make wild accusations?"

J.D. clenched his fists at his sides, wanting nothing more than to drive his knuckles straight into Rayburn's smirking face, but he didn't have time for revenge. He needed information, fast.

"Where did you send Natalie?"

Rayburn stared back, silent but smug. His expression reminded J.D. of the way Marlon Dyson had looked at the jail, almost gleeful about protecting the mysterious Alex.

How had Hamilton Gray purchased such loyalty? He had enough money to buy the county twice over, but the price for selling one's soul was surely higher than that, wasn't it?

"He's lured her somewhere," J.D. said aloud, fighting any show of fear. A sign of weakness would only strengthen Rayburn's resolve. He had to be the stronger horse. Alpha to Rayburn's beta. "He's going to kill her."

"I thought you liked Natalie." Massey couldn't hide his disgust. J.D. could only imagine how the deputy must feel, having worked side by side with Travis Rayburn for who knew how long without having a clue what he was really up to.

The phone on Massey's desk rang. He glanced at J.D. and grabbed it. "Massey."

"You know Marlon Dyson was murdered, don't you?" J.D. asked Rayburn quietly. "That's the loyalty Alex shows his partners."

"I heard he poisoned himself."

"Is that what you heard? Did you know about Victor Logan, too? How he blew up in a gas explosion Marlon set?"

Rayburn's eyes glittered with hidden satisfaction but he remained silent.

"You killed Dyson, didn't you? Or paid off someone to do it." J.D. shook his head. "That's how Hamilton does his dirty work, you know. Through his lackeys. But he won't let you kill the women for him. He's the only one who gets to do that."

"I thought you said I did kill for him," Rayburn shot back, his eyes glittering with a pride he couldn't conceal. "Lydia Randolph, I believe you said?"

"That's right. I'm sure you've read the case file. I can't imagine you'd have been able to resist the chance to gloat over your handiwork."

Massey hung up the phone. "Annabelle's," he barked. "She's headed to Annabelle's." He grabbed his jacket.

J.D. grabbed his arm. "I'll go." He lowered his voice. "Don't let Rayburn leave. He killed Lydia Randolph."

"Do you have proof?"

"Just keep him here. Try to keep him from making any phone calls, okay?"

"I'm sending backup!" Massey called as J.D. started for the exit, adrenaline pumping in his veins like fire.

As he reached the doorway, Rayburn called after him. "You're crazy, you know that?"

J.D. paused just long enough to turn and glare at Rayburn with stone cold fury. "And your friend is a dead man."

Then he raced for his truck, hoping he could stop Natalie from making a fatal mistake.

NATALIE WIPED THE perspiration from her brow and checked her watch. Eleven-forty and still no sign of her father. Was it possible he was already here? He could have had someone drop him off there, thinking he could get a ride back home with Natalie. It didn't seem like something her father would do, but since Carrie's murder, none of the Beckers were really acting like themselves, were they?

If he had a key—and knowing Carrie, she'd probably given her parents a copy—he might already be inside, waiting for her.

That meant she was late.

Reluctantly, she got out of the car and trudged up the flag-stone walkway to the restaurant's front door, wishing she'd just left her father a message to meet somewhere else. She tried the front lock and found it still engaged.

Pulling out her key, she opened the door and stepped inside. Even without air-conditioning, the restaurant was considerably cooler than the interior of her car.

"Hello?" she called, in case her father was in the back.

She listened carefully but heard no response. Still, she couldn't shake the sudden feeling that she wasn't alone in the restaurant.

Carrie, are you here? She didn't say the words aloud—that was a little too crazy even for her. But as she pulled down one of the chairs from the nearest table and settled to wait, she could almost feel her sister's spirit with her.

Natalie wished she could keep Carrie's dream alive, but she knew nothing about the restaurant business. Her best hope to honor Carrie was to find a buyer who loved the place as much as Carrie had and who'd breathe new life into the old building.

With a sigh, she stood up and walked to the front window, peering out into the bright sunlight. Still no sign of her father. She pulled her phone from her purse and checked for a message from her father.

The second the phone came on, it started to vibrate. J.D.'s name filled the display screen again.

With a sigh, she answered. "What's up, J.D.?"

"Thank God!" J.D. sounded almost hoarse with relief. "Listen, Natalie, you have to get out of Annabelle's. Get in your car and head straight to the police station."

She frowned. "How did you know where I am?"

He ignored the question. "You were right. Well, so was I, but—you were right about Hamilton Gray. He killed your sister."

She felt a flicker of satisfaction, quickly eclipsed by revulsion at the thought of Carrie's last moments being spent knowing that her husband, the man she'd loved beyond all reason, was going to kill her. "How do you know?"

As he outlined Hamilton's past as a stalker, Natalie's gut tightened with growing rage. How many people had known about his history? Terrebonne was a small town—he couldn't have stalked Brenda Teague without people knowing about it, could he?

"She didn't tell anyone? What about the Teagues?"

"They talked to his parents, tried to handle things quietly. Nobody's going to want to go against a family like the Grays."

What about her own family? Had her parents known Hamilton's little secret when they gave Carrie their blessing to marry him? Had his money trumped any of their concerns about his character?

"Your father didn't leave a message for you at the station. Are you out of the restaurant yet?"

She realized she hadn't made the first move to leave. "I'm leaving now—"

"I'm afraid you're not."

Natalie whirled around at the sound of the low, amused voice.

J.D.'s voice was urgent in her ear. "Natalie, are you out of the restaurant yet?"

It took a second for her eyes to adjust to the dim interior of the restaurant after so many minutes gazing outside at the bright day. But what she saw when her sight focused made her blood freeze.

Hamilton Gray stood a few feet away, smiling with wicked delight. In his right hand, he held a compact black Ruger.

And, tucked under his left arm, he held J.D.'s son, Mike.

"NATALIE?" HER SUDDEN silence on the other end of the line set J.D.'s nerves on edge. "Are you out of there?"

He heard a voice on the other end of the line. Not Natalie's. A male voice, indistinct but unmistakable.

Then the line went dead.

J.D. punched the resend button. The call went straight to voicemail. He growled a profanity under his breath and gunned the Ford's engine. But within moments, traffic along Sedge Road, that had never been heavy during J.D.'s stay in Terrebonne, drew to a crawl. Ahead, he saw flashing-blue lights. An accident?

The next turnoff was a half mile down the road, blocked by about two dozen cars between him and the side road. Behind him, traffic was already backing up, boxing him in. The shoulder wasn't wide enough to accommodate a motorcycle, much less his F-250. Worse, the slow crawl forward had come to a halt. He didn't even have room to pull a U-turn and head back up the road to the crossroads he'd just passed a few minutes earlier.

He tried Natalie's number again and got voicemail. Tamping down his rising fear, he searched his contacts for the Ridley County Sheriff's Department and asked for Doyle Massey. Massey answered on the second ring.

"I reached her on the phone but she hung up suddenly," J.D. told the deputy. "But I heard what sounded like a man's voice over the line before she cut off. Now I can't reach her, and I'm stuck in some sort of traffic jam on Sedge Road."

"On Sedge?" Massey sounded surprised. "Is it an accident?"

"I see blue lights ahead, but I can't see a crash." J.D. tried to see past a tall delivery truck a few vehicles ahead of him on the road. "I can't even pull a U-turn—I'm boxed in."

"I called in a backup unit for you—you should see them on the road behind you somewhere."

J.D. checked his rear view mirror. "I don't see anything."

"I'll call and see where they are—"

"Wait—where's Rayburn?"

"He lawyered up. Union lawyer's on the way, so he's cooling his heels in one of the interview rooms."

"Are you sure he's still there?"

"I'm looking at the door right now. No other way out."

The car ahead of J.D. inched forward as the traffic started to move, giving J.D. just enough room to cut left into a U-turn. "I'm making the U-turn. I'll call you once I hit the crossroads and you tell me the best way to Annabelle's from there."

"Okay. I'll see what's keeping your backup."

J.D. hung up and wheeled the truck around until he was headed back up Sedge Road in the opposite direction. As he neared the crossroads, he called Massey. "County Road 6. Left or right?"

"Take a right, then the first right on Lombard. It'll parallel Sedge to County Road 9. Take a right there and you'll hit a crossroads with Sedge a quarter mile up from the restaurant. I've checked in with the backup. The traffic snarl is from a road block—apparently the department got a tip about someone carrying a load of stolen pseudoephedrine heading down Sedge Road."

"Called in when?"

"About an hour ago."

"About the time Natalie got the mysterious message?"

Massey was silent a moment, then growled a profanity.

"Get the backup to Annabelle's however they have to do it."

"I'll see if I can track them down and reroute. All the other units are out on calls."

J.D. hung up and took a right at County Road 6, praying he wasn't too late.

Chapter Sixteen

"Put the gun down, Natalie." Hamilton pressed the barrel of his pistol into the side of Mike's temple, making the boy gasp.

Natalie had never doubted his treachery, not since she'd found her sister dead and knew, bone-deep, that Hamilton was behind it. But until this moment, she hadn't really realized just how truly depraved he was. He might pretend he was trading Mike's life for her cooperation, but Natalie knew he couldn't afford to let either of them out of here alive. The only thing her cooperation might afford either of them was a little more time.

"The gun?" Hamilton prodded.

But a little more time was better than nothing. A little more time might give her the chance to come up with a way to save J.D.'s son's life as well as her own. Slowly, she took her Smith & Wesson from the holster at her hip and laid it on the floor.

"Kick it over here."

She did as Hamilton asked, locking gazes with Mike. The kid looked terrified, but he also looked angry as hell, reminding her of his father.

Hamilton kicked her gun across the room. It skittered behind the cashier's desk, hitting the wall with a low thud.

"He won't let us live," Mike said. "We already know what he looks like."

"Natalie knows who I am," Hamilton corrected with a smile.

"I think he's the one who killed my mom," Mike said urgently.

"I know," Natalie said, everything starting to make sense. "You're the infamous Alex, aren't you?"

Hamilton's smile widened, making him look like a snarling wolf. "You always were so much brighter than your sister."

"Don't you dare speak of my sister."

"What—you don't want to know all the gory details of what I did to her? Or why?" His smile faded, though an expression of cruel amusement remained on his face. "I thought she was dim and malleable, you know. It's why I married her. I needed a wife at my age. She stopped the vile questions about my manhood."

"What manhood?" Natalie kept her eye on his trigger finger. Though his finger was off the trigger, a twitch could fire a shot.

Hamilton's eyes darkened. "What would a sexless crone like you know about manhood?"

"I know real men don't get their jollies with knives. They use what God gave 'em."

To Natalie's surprise, Mike's lips curved in a smile of satisfaction at her taunt. What a tough little kid.

"She didn't suspect a thing until she started talking to you," Hamilton continued, ignoring her words. "Maybe if I'd killed you first, I wouldn't have had to kill her until much later on. Does that make you feel guilty?"

"Only that I didn't figure out what a sick bastard you were soon enough to save the other women you've killed."

"I considered marrying you instead of Carrie. Did you know that? But when I thought about having to sleep with a frigid little fishwife like you, I just couldn't do it."

"You didn't go after me because you know I find you repulsive," Natalie countered with a sharp smile. "Carrie always saw the good in people, even when it didn't exist. And you swept her off her romantic little feet, just as I'm sure you planned. But I'm not a romantic. Neither was Brenda Cooper, was she?"

"Brenda Teague," Hamilton corrected. "She only married that brainless ox because her parents had poisoned her mind against me and made her feel afraid."

Natalie saw Mike's face crease with fury a split second before he moved, giving her no time to warn him off. The boy jabbed his elbow hard into Hamilton's groin, catching the man completely off guard.

Hamilton doubled over with a howl of pain, his gun hand dropping enough to free Mike from his grasp.

"Run!" Natalie yelled at the boy, though her warning was unnecessary. Mike was already halfway to the door before Hamilton could react. He started running after the boy, raising his gun.

Natalie hit Hamilton at a run, slamming him to the ground. She went for the Ruger but he backhanded her with the butt of the gun, knocking her flying. He aimed wildly in her direction.

She scrambled backward toward the kitchen, making it through the swinging door as a gunshot split the air. The round hit the door with a splintering thunk.

She gazed around, spotting an old freestanding dishwasher tucked against the wall nearby. It wasn't as heavy as she'd like, but she shoved it in front of the swinging door, ducking behind the unit as another round splintered the door.

Scrambling toward the back of the kitchen through a maze of old appliances, she realized she'd never reach the back door before Hamilton pushed past the obstacle she'd put in his path. There was a quicker path to the window to her left, and it was already open—was that how Mike had ended up in Hamilton's grasp?

The door behind her started to bang against the dishwasher, scraping it forward slowly but surely.

She couldn't make it to the window in time. Even if she could reach it before he made it into the kitchen, she'd be a sitting duck going over the sill. Instead, she took cover behind a massive old double stove, panic rising in smothering waves. She forced herself to keep her breathing low and soft as Hamilton's footsteps entered the kitchen. He moved slowly. Deliberately.

His low chuckle filled the thick silence. "Come out, come out, wherever you are," he called in a singsong voice.

Stay calm, Becker. You're still alive. There's still hope. Mike was safely out of the restaurant, right? He'd go get help.

But how could anyone reach her in time?

J.D. PARKED THE TRUCK a few yards down the road from Annabelle's, hidden from view of the restaurant, and circled around through the woods behind the building. He had almost made it to the edge of the woods when he heard a low, urgent whisper nearby. "Dad!"

He turned his head and found himself staring into the terrified brown eyes of his son, who was crouched nearby behind a scrubby, wild hydrangea bush.

J.D. hurried to his son's side, his heart hammering against his ribs. "What are you doing here, Mike?"

"Get down! He's inside!"

J.D. crouched by his son. "Who?"

"He says his name is Hamilton, but Natalie called him Alex, and he said he knew Mom and I think maybe he killed her. He has a gun, and I heard shots—"

J.D.'s breath froze. "How many?"

"Two, I think. Maybe three—I'm not sure about one of them."

"Where were they coming from?"

"I think I heard it coming from the kitchen."

"What happened, Mike?"

His son told him about falling right into Hamilton Gray's grasp the second he went through the back window, then about Natalie's arrival and what had transpired next. "He was talking about you and Mom and said she didn't really want to marry you, that her parents just scared her into it, and it made me really mad, so I jabbed my elbow in his privates and ran away."

Pride battled with terror as he realized how close he'd come to losing his son. "How did you get here in the first place?"

"I borrowed Derek's bike," he confessed, looking miserable.

"Okay, here's what I want you to do. My truck is parked just down the road." J.D. pointed in the direction where he'd left the vehicle. "Take my phone, go lock yourself in the truck and call the last number I dialed on the phone. Ask for Deputy Massey and tell him everything that's happened. Tell him to get the backup here if he has to fly it in."

"I don't want to leave you," Mike whispered desperately.

J.D. caught his son's face between his hands. "I need you to do this for me, Mike. There's no more time to wait. I'm trusting you to get the backup here. I know you can do it. Okay?"

Tears welled in Mike's eyes, but he nodded. "I can do it."

J.D. kissed Mike's forehead, his heart breaking. "I love you. Go now."

"I love you, Daddy." Mike sniffed back his tears, pushed to his feet and started running through the woods at a sprint.

J.D. wanted to watch his son to safety, but he was running out of time. He had to get to the restaurant and find out what was happening to Natalie. Mike had said Hamilton had kicked Natalie's gun across the room. Had she had time to reach it after Mike's diversion? Were some of the gunshots hers?

He couldn't assume so. He had to assume she was still unarmed, maybe injured. Or worse.

His mind rebelled at the thought, threatening to paralyze him. He forced the worst-case scenario out of his mind. Natalie was still alive. She had to be.

He stayed low, approaching the restaurant at a corner angle, where he wouldn't be immediately visible through the back windows. Spotting the open window Mike had mentioned, he ran at a crouch, staying below the line of sight.

A man's voice filtered through the window. "When I find you, I'll kill you. And it won't be an easy death. But if you'll come out now without any fuss, I'll make it quick and clean."

Only silence answered Hamilton Gray's offer. Natalie was too smart to engage with Gray and give him a better idea where she was hiding, J.D. knew. But how long could she hold out before Gray finally tracked down her hiding spot?

J.D. didn't dare take a peek inside the kitchen. He'd be an easy target if Gray was looking toward the open window.

Think, Cooper.

He glanced down the back wall of the restaurant, counting the windows. Six total—two flanking the door and four a bit farther down. At least two would belong to customer bathrooms. Was there a staff bathroom? That might account for the other windows.

He crept toward the other windows and looked inside. The nearest window past the kitchen was a storeroom. The one after that seemed to be the staff bathroom. He could see a sink and a single toilet, and beyond that a door that probably led into the store room.

He looked up at the latch. It was locked.

He'd have to break the window if he wanted in. Was the

store room far enough from the kitchen that the breaking glass wouldn't draw Hamilton's attention?

He heard Hamilton Gray's voice drifting through the open window nearby. "What, no questions, Natalie? Don't you want to know why I do what I do?"

You do what you do because you like it, you deviant bastard, J.D. thought, an idea forming as he gazed at the window overhead.

He scanned the ground until he found what he was looking for—a large rock, about the size of a baseball. Heaving it as hard as he could, he threw the rock through the employee's bathroom window. The glass shattered loudly, eliciting a curse from Hamilton Gray in the kitchen.

J.D. crept to the open window and sat, waiting for Gray to respond. One of two things would happen: either he'd go check on the broken window, which would require him to go through two doors, leaving the kitchen empty for a crucial few seconds; or he'd look out the open window for who threw the rock.

Either way, J.D. would be ready for him.

He was hoping for the latter option. The second Gray's face appeared in the window, he'd catch him unaware from below the window. It could be over in seconds.

But, of course, Gray chose the other option.

"Do you think you can reach either door before I can get back here and shoot you?" Gray asked aloud, his voice already moving toward the side of the kitchen where the door to the store room must be. "I rather hope you give it a try. But I've blocked the door to the front, and there's no way to open the back door without a key—and I'll hear the rattle."

Natalie didn't respond, but J.D. could almost feel her, somewhere just inside, weighing her options.

J.D. dared a quick look through the window and saw Hamilton Gray's back disappear through the store room door.

He had no time to waste. As silently as possible, he hauled himself through the open window and dropped to the floor.

SHE'D HAVE SECONDS, TOPS. Her weapon was behind the cashier's desk at the front of the restaurant, which made the swinging door the most tempting target. But an obstacle course of old kitchen appliances stood between her and freedom. The back door would require a key—could she get her keys out of her pocket without making a rattle? Unlikely.

That left the open window behind her.

She turned and looked at the window, which was only a few yards away, though a half freezer stood between her and her best hope of escape.

Suddenly, someone rose up over the window sill, filling the entire space for a second, then dropped silently to the ground.

She had to blink a couple of times to be certain she was seeing what she thought. J.D. stared back at her, his eyes full of deadly determination. Then he disappeared again, soundlessly.

She listened for any sounds, but only the faintest scraping noise came from behind the freezer.

J.D. appeared again, rounding the side of the freezer on his hands and knees. He scooted forward until he was right beside her. "Are you okay?" he asked, making almost no sound.

"Fine," she assured him, equally quiet. "Mike—"

"He's okay." He showed her the gun tucked into the waistband of his jeans. "I need you to distract him. Head for the window. Make some noise." He caught her face between his big hands, making her feel strangely invincible. He bent and kissed her, hard and fast.

"Good luck." He let her go, shifting to a better position to see the door to the store room.

Natalie scooted toward the window, not bothering to be

quiet. She heard Hamilton moving back toward the kitchen, but she didn't let herself turn and look at his position.

J.D. had her back. He wouldn't let anything happen.

J.D. PEERED AROUND THE side of the ovens, watching the store room door for Hamilton Gray's return. He heard the footsteps, moving at a clip, and yet it seemed to take forever for the man to make his way through the door.

In one fluid movement, J.D. rose to his feet and leveled his SIG at Hamilton Gray's center mass. He opened his mouth to order Gray to drop the Ruger. What came out, however, was, "Make a wrong move. Please. Just one little twitch."

Natalie's soft gasp faintly registered, but he kept his focus firmly on Gray, whose wide green eyes stared back at him with complete shock. He froze in place, not moving, though a muscle in his jaw clenched and unclenched.

"I'm putting down my gun," Gray said after a long, tense moment, slowly lifting his free hand and dropping the barrel of his Ruger until it pointed at the floor. "Nice and easy here. No tricks." He bent to the ground slowly, lowering the gun.

No, J.D. thought. *It can't just end like this. It can't be this easy for the bastard.*

He watched carefully, hoping Gray would make a wrong move, anything to give him an excuse to shoot. An excuse he could live with. But Gray seemed to know exactly what J.D. wanted from him, and he was careful to give him nothing at all. No resistance. No twitchy moves. Not even a mocking retort.

"Kick the gun over here to me." Natalie rose from her hiding place near the window.

Gray cocked his head slightly, a faint smile on his face as he complied. J.D. found the smile so profane, under the circumstances, that his finger trembled on the trigger. It was all he could do to cling to his dwindling sense of control.

He could picture the outcome so clearly it made his head

ache. Hamilton Gray would give himself up. Cop to taking Natalie hostage and pretend he'd snapped out of grief for his dead wife and Natalie's constant accusations and harassment. If he'd chosen Travis Rayburn wisely, the man would keep his mouth shut, even if the police could somehow connect him to Lydia Randolph's murder, and there'd be nothing to connect Gray to any of the murders, including Brenda's.

Eventually, he'd be loose again. He'd kill again.

Natalie took Gray's Ruger from the floor a foot in front of her. "Facedown on the floor. Legs spread, hands above your head. Now!"

As Gray started to comply, J.D. barked, "No!"

Gray froze again. He and Natalie both turned to look at J.D.

J.D.'s gun leveled with Gray's heart again. "He'll walk. You know he will. We can't prove anything we know."

Natalie's eyes widened with alarm. "J.D., he's surrendered—I can testify—"

"You can tell them he kidnapped you. But everybody knows you wanted to prove he killed your sister. Anything he told you here is your word against his." J.D. felt as if a cold, black flood had filled his body until he was drowning in it.

Drowning in hate. Sinking into the dark heart of blood vengeance.

This son of a bitch had killed his wife. Took his children's mother from them. Took his in-laws' child from them. Took away the woman J.D. had planned to love for a long, happy lifetime.

He'd killed other women. Other daughters, mothers, wives. And J.D. could end it now, so easily. One pull of the trigger. One bullet tearing through Gray's chest to stop his black heart.

"If you do this, he wins. He's a destroyer." Natalie's voice was low but relentless, buzzing in his head, cutting through the darkness gathering there. "You're not a destroyer, J.D.

You're a father. You're a son. You're a brother. You'll leave a big damned hole in this world, and he'll have won. It'll be his last act, but he'll have won."

Gray looked from Natalie back to J.D., his eyes bright with consternation. *He wants me to shoot him,* J.D. realized. *He wants me to be his last big conquest.*

He felt Natalie's hand on his shoulder, her touch careful, gentle. It was as if a band of tension snapped, releasing him from the force of his rage. The blackness drained away, leaving him feeling light-headed.

"On the ground," he growled at Gray. "Legs spread, hands behind your head."

Gray almost wilted with disappointment. Slowly, he dropped to the ground, complying with J.D.'s order.

Beside J.D., Natalie exhaled softly. "I hear sirens."

J.D. nodded, keeping his gun trained on Gray's back but no longer overwhelmed by the urge to pull the trigger.

Backup had arrived, just in time.

J.D. GRIMACED WITH frustration as the backup officers took his statement, looking around for Massey. He'd tried to tell the responding officers that his son was out there in the woods, probably scared out of his mind waiting to hear word of J.D.'s fate, but other than offering a vague promise to check on him as soon as possible, the deputies seemed far less worried than J.D. about his son's safety, much less his state of mind. They'd taken Gray into custody, and they seemed a little unsure whether they had enough evidence to keep him there.

Natalie intervened, finally, as if she sensed his growing impatience. "J.D. got here late. He can't add much. Let him go find his son."

Giving her a silent look of gratitude, J.D. headed out the front door of the restaurant.

He ran into Massey on his way inside. "Did Mike get you?" J.D. asked.

Massey looked confused. "Mike?"

"My son. I sent him to the truck to call you and let you know we'd found Natalie with Gray. Gray had taken him hostage—"

"He took your son hostage?"

J.D.'s chest tightened painfully. "He didn't call you?"

Massey shook his head.

J.D. didn't wait to explain. He set off through the woods at a dead run. By the time he made it to his truck, he heard a couple of footsteps pounding through the woods behind him, but there was no time to waste checking which of the deputies had taken chase. He found the sheltered turnoff where he'd left the truck and relaxed for a half second when he saw it was still where he'd parked it. But he faltered to a stop when he went around to the truck cab. It was empty. But the windshield wasn't.

Five crude red swooshes, loosely forming the shape of a shark's head, marred the glass. Every drop of blood in J.D.'s veins turned to ice as he stared at the mark.

Please, God, please don't let it be blood. Please.

As he stepped forward to touch the mark, the people who'd been chasing him through the woods caught up. He heard their rapid breathing, even heard Massey call out, "Don't touch it!" But he had to know. Now.

He touched the damp mark and drew his fingertip to his nose. The pungent smell of latex paint burned his nose.

He felt his knees begin to wobble and he slumped against the side of the truck, his pulse thundering in his ears.

"J.D., is that—?" Natalie's voice penetrated the noise in his head, and he turned to look at her. She was staring at the red mark. "Is it blood?"

"Paint," he rasped.

"But it's their mark, isn't it?" She dragged her gaze away from the mark and met his eyes, her face pale and her eyes wide and haunted. *"Los Tiburones."*

Behind her, Massey uttered a profanity.

J.D. nodded, as afraid as he could ever remember being. "Eladio Cordero's thugs have my son."

Chapter Seventeen

"We've got a perimeter set up in the county—every law enforcement agency available. The feds are already on their way from Mobile, and they're sending agents from Birmingham, too—"

J.D. whirled on Massey, his eyes wild. "It's been at least a half an hour! If they hit I-10, they could be in another state!"

Natalie put her hand on his arm, but he shrugged off her touch. The look of terror in his face made her stomach ache.

"We've contacted the contiguous states as well, plus—"

A ringing sound interrupted Massey's attempt at further reassurance. "That's my phone," J.D. said, looking around wildly.

Natalie spotted it on the ground a few feet behind the truck and bent to pick it up.

"Don't touch it—it's evidence," Massey called.

J.D. gave the deputy a black look and grabbed the phone. His brow furrowed. "My brother Luke."

"The one Cordero's really after?" Natalie murmured.

He nodded and engaged the phone. "What is it?" He listened a second, then his gaze shot up and locked with Natalie's, dread shining like black ice behind his eyes. "I'm putting you on speaker. There are people here who need to hear this."

A second later, Natalie heard the roar of what sounded like a loud engine and a man's voice, shouting to be heard over the noise. "Cordero called maybe thirty minutes ago. It was Cordero himself, not one of his goons, and he put Mike on the phone."

Natalie felt as if her heart had twisted into a knot right in the center of her chest, making it nearly impossible to breathe.

"He wants to trade Mike for me. I'm on my way down there."

"I'm not trading you for Mike," J.D. insisted, starting to pace. "I'm going to find that drug-running son of a bitch and kill him myself."

Natalie glanced at Massey for her colleague's reaction. To her surprise—and relief—Massey didn't seem bothered by J.D.'s rant. She wished she could be as sanguine about the return of J.D.'s bloodlust. She'd been relieved when the showdown at the restaurant had ended without any further felonies.

"No, you're not," Luke said. "He wants me. He won't kill Mike because I told him I'm not doing a damned thing he tells me until I talk to Mike again. Mike's a tool, not a goal."

"He wants to kill us all, Luke!" The despair in J.D.'s voice was raw and affecting. Natalie tried to touch his arm again. This time, he let her hand remain, though understandably, he noticed it no more than he'd notice a fly landing on his shoulder.

"I know that, but he won't kill Mike until he's no longer useful," Luke responded. "And we've got about an hour to figure out how to find him before that happens."

"You're in a bird?" J.D. asked.

"Billy at the heliport's flying us for free. You know he

thinks the world of Mike, and he has combat training." Luke's voice darkened. "We may need it."

"Who else is with you?" J.D. asked.

"Gabe, Jake and Sam. The others stayed back in Gossamer Ridge—they're gathering the family at the lake house and getting as much local LEO support as they can on short notice, in case this is a diversionary tactic and they're the real target."

"I hope that'll be enough," J.D. said grimly.

"Uncle Roy's kids are coming over from Maybridge to help set up the perimeter. All except Rick. He's down in your neck of the woods on a case for Cooper Security. He should be calling you soon to figure out a rendezvous point."

"What's your ETA?"

"Around fourteen hundred," Luke answered, his call starting to break up. "We've hit a bad coverage spot—I'll call back—" The line went dead.

J.D. growled with frustration. "How the hell did Cordero find Mike out here in the middle of nowhere? I didn't even know my son was here until thirty minutes ago."

"Oh my God," Natalie whispered, a terrible idea beginning to take hold in her mind.

Both Massey and J.D. turned to look at her. "What?"

"Hamilton," she said. "I couldn't figure out why he was holding Mike in the first place. But if he'd made a deal—"

J.D. frowned. "With Cordero? Why? For that matter—how?"

"Gray Global Partners has a huge import/export operation headquartered in Tesoro." For Massey's sake, she added, "Sanselmo's capital city."

"I guess to do business there, you have to rub elbows with a lot of shady people," Massey commented.

"Hard to avoid," Natalie agreed. She turned to J.D. "And what if that shooting at the motel was meant for you instead of me? Hamilton may have called Cordero in as soon as he

found out you were hanging around town asking questions—
what if it was a dry run to send you a message or maybe even
an outright attempt on your life? What if I just got in the
way?"

For the first time since he'd discovered his son missing, J.D.
seemed to really see Natalie. He lifted his hand as if he were
about to touch her face. But he dropped his arm to his side
and turned away. She could feel him distancing himself, inch
by inch. "Did he make any calls while you were there?"

"No, but he had Mike before I ever went in the restaurant.
He could have made a call at any point before that."

"We can find out," Massey said.

She and J.D. both looked at the deputy.

"We have Gray in custody," he reminded them. "That
means we have his phone."

J.D. RODE WITH NATALIE to the police station, since the sheriff's department considered his truck a crime scene. It was the
first chance he'd had to be alone with her since those brief,
stolen moments crouched behind the stove in the restaurant
kitchen. But hell if he knew what to say.

He could see her growing sense of insecurity as he kept
up the silent treatment, and a part of him hated himself for
doing something that obviously hurt her, after all that she'd
done to help him and his son.

But if this recent, horrific turn of events proved anything,
it was that it could be very dangerous to be involved with a
Cooper as long as Eladio Cordero was alive. His brothers and
sister had somehow made peace with the threats, pushed, no
doubt, by their headstrong partners.

But J.D. had lost too much in his life already. He'd be
damned if he let Natalie Becker get killed for no reason other
than her relationship with him.

"If we can prove Hamilton called Eladio Cordero or one

of his associates," Natalie murmured, "it may not matter that we can't yet prove his connection to the serial killings."

"It should be enough to keep him in jail a good, long time, even with his money and connections," J.D. agreed, but only halfheartedly, because he was beginning to wonder if Gray would ever really get what was coming to him.

"One way or the other, I'll connect him to these cases," Natalie vowed, her voice low and fervent. "If I don't do anything else in my life but that, it will have been a worthwhile life."

J.D.'s cell phone rang. When he saw the unfamiliar number, his heart began to race. He answered. "Cooper."

"Same here," came a low voice he hadn't heard in years. "Rick."

"You hanging in there, J.D.?" his cousin asked.

"Yeah, for the moment. Luke said you were in the area and wanted to help?"

"I'm nearly in Terrebonne—tell me where to meet you." His cousin sounded calm and unperturbed, something J.D. might have found annoying if he didn't know Rick had spent the last six years as a security consultant in every hell hole in South America, Africa, Europe, Asia and the Middle East. There probably wasn't a thing that would make him blink at this point in his life.

"I'm heading to the Ridley County Sheriff's Department. Know where that is?"

"On my way." Rick hung up.

"Was that the cousin your brother mentioned?"

J.D. nodded. "He'll be good in a fight."

Natalie let him off at the door and went to find a parking place, apparently aware he wouldn't want to waste a minute. J.D. went inside and found a deputy waiting for him. "Deputy Massey said to bring you straight back."

Massey was in a small room off the deputies' bullpen, where he watched as another deputy slit open a bag containing what J.D. presumed were Hamilton Gray's personal effects. Massey looked up at J.D.'s arrival. "Good—just in time. Where's Natalie?"

"Parking," J.D. answered. "Don't wait. She'll catch up."

Massey nodded to the other deputy, who opened Gray's cell phone. "We dragged a judge away from lunch at The Magnolia to sign the warrant, but we got it."

J.D. knew he should care—building a case against Gray was vital—but even without a warrant, he wouldn't have left this room until he knew what was on that phone.

"There was a call placed to a number about an hour ago."

That would track with the time Mike was at the restaurant, J.D. thought.

After the deputy checked the number on a nearby computer, he looked up at Massey glumly. "Disposable cell."

Massey glanced at J.D. "Could be a coincidence."

"No." J.D. pulled out his own phone and called Luke.

Luke answered, his voice still raised over the helicopter engine. "J.D., we're just over Ridley County now. We've been cleared to land at the Sheriff's Department—"

"That's where I am now," J.D. interrupted. "Listen—did you track the number Eladio Cordero used to call you?"

"It's got to be a disposable—"

"I know, but do you have the number?"

"Let me look." After a second, Luke rattled off a number.

J.D. looked at the deputy at the computer. He looked away from the screen and nodded.

"Son of a bitch," J.D. growled.

"What is it?" Luke asked.

"We know who tipped Cordero off."

"Who?"

"The man who killed Brenda."

THE NEXT HOUR WAS A whirlwind, filled with Coopers descending on the sheriff's department helipad within seconds of the arrival of J.D.'s cousin Rick, a tall, dark-haired man with coffee-brown eyes who looked enough like J.D. and his brothers that Natalie knew he was a Cooper before he ever stepped out of the big black Ford Expedition he drove.

The Coopers didn't linger, staying long enough for Natalie to meet them all and for J.D. to tell her about the phone call from Hamilton to Eladio Cordero. They piled into the Expedition and headed off, leaving Natalie to shove her feelings into her pocket and do the only thing she could.

Talk Massey into letting her speak to Hamilton Gray alone.

Gray had the audacity to smile at her when she entered the interrogation room. She swallowed her nausea and sat across from him, taking comfort—and a little bit of mean pleasure—at the sight of shackles on his wrists and ankles.

"I really shouldn't be talking to you without my lawyer."

"He can be here if you like. I'm still going to ask you questions." Natalie didn't like the light in Hamilton's eyes at her response, but she pushed on. "Here's what we know. Less than an hour before Mike Cooper was abducted by Eladio Cordero's thugs, you made a phone call to his disposable cell phone from yours."

"I called a golfing buddy who doesn't like cell contracts."

"Eladio Cordero called Luke Cooper from the same disposable cell number and put Mike on the phone to speak to his uncle."

Hamilton's eyes twitched.

"You were going to give Mike to them. That was why you were calling. That's why they were out in the woods waiting. When he ran away, they grabbed him." She leaned closer to him. "What was the trade-off? You give them Mike, they kill J.D. for you?"

Hamilton pressed his mouth to a tight line.

"You must really hate him for taking Brenda away. So unworthy of her. So inferior to you." Natalie choked the words out through a haze of loathing. "Right?"

"He's certainly inferior," Hamilton agreed coolly.

"You spent a year flying back and forth to Sanselmo as a liaison for your father's company eight years ago." Natalie made a mental note to see if there were any unsolved murders in Tesoro fitting the profile of his other murders. "Did you have to make deals with *El Cambio?* With the cartels?"

"You think your daddy's never made any deals with the devil?"

"I know he has," she answered flatly. "When did you call them to come here?"

"You think Eladio Cordero doesn't have eyes and ears everywhere?" Hamilton asked. "Even here?"

His tone set off alarm bells in Natalie's head. He wasn't talking generally about Terrebonne. He was talking about the Sheriff's Department. "Who?"

"I don't know. I don't care. It has nothing to do with me, as I continue to explain to you."

There was a knock on the door behind her. She got up and went outside, where she found Massey frowning at her. "He's saying we've got a Cordero plant here at the department?"

She started to nod, then looked up at Massey, trying to look at him with as objective an eye as she could. What did she really know about him, anyway? He'd suddenly started being friendly after he'd interviewed J.D. about the trespassing charge. Was he playing nice to keep a closer eye on J.D.?

He'd been the first to respond to the drive-by shooting. He knew where J.D. was most of the time, because he'd had good reason to keep tabs on them both after the shooting attempt.

"If you think it's me, take a look at my records jacket," Massey said grimly. "My brother, David, worked as a relief worker in Sanselmo during the cartel riots seven years ago. Cordero and his monsters wiped out the whole camp. They found David in pieces. All the kid wanted to do was help people, and they slaughtered him like a dog." His jaw clenched. "If you think I'd do anything but shoot the bastard dead if I saw him, you're barking up the wrong tree."

She studied his reaction, gauged his sincerity. The rage and pain in his eyes couldn't be faked. "Okay. But who else has been connected to this case? Could it be Travis Rayburn?"

"Maybe," Massey said.

"Who were the deputies who picked up J.D. at the restaurant that time I called in the tip?"

"Dusty and Joy."

Natalie dismissed the idea of Joy Allen being the contact—Cordero and his ilk were notoriously chauvinistic. They'd never trust an American woman as an informant. Nor could she see what might tempt Joy, who was a newlywed with a good-looking husband who worked a high-paying job at a Mobile investment bank.

"Dusty's kid is sick," Massey murmured. "Some autoimmune thing. His insurance covers a lot, but there are a lot of things it doesn't." Massey frowned. "That's why he took the security job at the charity fundraiser at your folks' house."

"He was with you when you responded to the drive-by, wasn't he?" At Massey's nod, her heart sank. "I need to know where Cordero would take Mike to hide him. And if Dusty knows—"

"We'll find out," Massey said grimly.

J.D. REALIZED IT HAD been nearly six years since he'd last seen his cousin Rick at a Christmas family get-together. The years between had taken a toll on his younger cousin, adding lines and hollows to his boyish face and a permanent watchfulness to his dark eyes. He'd worked for a security company called MacLear, a formerly well-respected company that, unbeknownst to most of its legitimate employees, had been running a hidden division that had acted as the personal army for a corrupt and dangerous State Department official.

J.D. had long suspected MacLear had a seamy underbelly, but Rick hadn't listened to his warning. One of the first things he did when J.D. slid into the front passenger seat of the Expedition was apologize. "I should've listened to you about MacLear."

"You didn't do anything wrong. A few criminals in your company did."

"Maybe you could tell that to Jesse," Rick murmured.

"He's your big brother. Busting your chops is his job."

"Yeah, just ask J.D." Gabe slid into the SUV behind them, Jake on his heels. They took the back bench seat, leaving the middle seats for Luke and Sam.

J.D. looked over his shoulder at his brothers, overwhelmed by the sudden sense of strength that came from just having them here. For the first time since seeing the mark of *Los Tiburones* on his windshield, J.D. felt as if they'd get Mike back alive.

"When Luke called me, I started calling some people I dealt with during my security jobs in Sanselmo. I got a call just before I arrived confirming that Cordero left Sanselmo about four or five days ago."

Just before the shots fired at his motel. J.D. told the others about the incident. "It was a pretty anemic attack."

"You're not his primary target," Luke reminded him. "It may have been more like a shot across the bow to let you know they're in town and they're watching. Maybe they hoped to leave a bigger message but your friend Natalie got in the way."

"Girlfriend Natalie?" Jake asked hopefully.

J.D. ignored him. "Mike was running around here for days and they didn't bother him."

"If Gray called them, it might have been too perfect an opportunity to ignore," Luke said. "If Cordero knows anything about me after all this time, it's that I'll go the distance to protect my family."

"Where to?" Rick asked.

"Right now, I want to go back to the woods where he disappeared," J.D. answered. "The locals will be there processing the scene around my truck, but I was thinking—Mike knows as much about leaving a bread-crumb trail in the woods as any of us did as kids, and we knew a hell of a lot."

"Think he may lead us to him?" Sam asked.

"It's worth a shot," J.D. answered. Mike had grown up in the woods around Gossamer Lake, playing for hours with his sister and other kids who lived in houses on the lake. Jake and Gabe had taken him on mountain hikes and taught him what they knew about tracking and survival.

Mike knew how to leave a trail so he could find his way back home, no matter how far he roamed. And from what Natalie had told him about his son's escape from Hamilton Gray, his kid was pretty tough and focused even when things were falling apart around him.

Show me where they took you, son. Give me a sign, and I'll follow as long as it takes.

IF MIKE COOPER HADN'T been in grave danger, Natalie might have felt sorry for Dusty Devlin. The young deputy cracked like an egg on the first question, clearly torn apart by what he'd done. "I swear, I didn't know who he was. He just said his name was Tomás, and he needed someone to help him keep an eye on Doc Teague. I didn't know why."

"How much did he pay you?" Massey asked.

"Two thousand a month." Devlin slanted a bleak look at Natalie. "I know it's a small price to sell your soul—"

"It paid the hospital bills?" Massey asked.

Devlin nodded. "Things were so bad, we were talking about letting the state take our daughter—we couldn't keep up with the bills, no matter how many hours I took on or how much the insurance covered. Janet can't work—Nina needs to be watched twenty-four/seven, and the price of a private nurse would eat up anything Janet could make—" He buried his face in his hands. "I'm sorry. I'm so sorry. I just needed the money so badly—"

Natalie exchanged a look with Massey, who looked sick. She couldn't blame him. Later, when she found Mike and knew he was safe, she'd find a way to help Dusty and his wife, but right now, she had to concentrate on J.D.'s son. "Does Tomás live here?"

"I don't know. I meet him out on Route 8 near Hansbury, first Thursday every month. Since January."

"What information have you given him?" Natalie asked.

"Nothing he couldn't find out at Margo's, I swear. I told him when the Teagues' grandkids came to visit. I told him their daddy is in town—I told him about that shooting—" Devlin looked wildly from Natalie to Massey, alarm darkening in his eyes. "Was he behind the shooting? Oh, God, please tell me he wasn't—"

"We don't know," Massey answered honestly. "But I think he's behind the kidnapping of the Teagues' grandson."

Devlin turned pale. Natalie grabbed a nearby trash can and set it in front of Devlin just before he threw up.

"Route 8 near Hansbury—why does that sound familiar to me?" Massey murmured as they waited out Devlin's nausea.

"It's mostly wilderness from there to the county line, but—" Natalie cut off short, sucking in a quick gasp. "The abandoned Gray Trading Company warehouse is out there. Probably swallowed by kudzu by now, but if Hamilton Gray's part of this whole mix—"

"That might be where he'd hide a bunch of South American, drug-cartel thugs," Massey finished for her.

"I've got to go." She waved at Devlin, who'd emptied his

stomach and now sat moaning at the interview table. "See if you can get anything more out of him."

"Don't you dare go anywhere without backup, Becker!"

Natalie waved as she hurried from the room, not ready to promise anything.

She had a feeling extreme stealth might be the only thing that could help Mike Cooper now.

Chapter Eighteen

J.D.'s phone vibrated against his hip. He pulled it out and saw Natalie's number in the display. "Anything from Gray?"

"No, but we have a new direction to look." She told him about a deputy on the take named Devlin and the abandoned warehouse off Route 8. "Where are you now?"

"Hitting a dead end," he admitted, glancing at the others. "Mike tried to leave us a trail to follow, but it ended on County Road 12. We're pretty sure they had a vehicle waiting here."

"Get in the car and go west on County Road 12—it'll take you right to Hansbury Crossroads. Take a right on Route 8 and circle north until you reach the old entrance to Gray Trading Company. That was the old distribution center for Gray Global Partners before they went public and started expanding their territory. The place has been abandoned for years, but it may still have enough structures standing to be a pretty good hideout for a bunch of people used to living in the Sanselmo jungle."

"What are you going to do?"

"Come in from the south." Natalie lowered her voice to an intense half whisper. "Be careful. Don't do anything to spook them. They're holding a hell of a lot of cards."

"They're holding the only card that matters," J.D. growled. "My son. I'll be careful. But I want you out of this."

"Hell, no."

"Natalie, it's done. You've been a great help to me, more than I can ever repay, but it's time for you to go back to your life and stop worrying about mine."

Natalie was silent for a moment, and J.D. knew he'd hurt her. But if that's what it took to make her go as far away from *Los Tiburones* and Eladio Cordero as possible, he could live with that.

"I have to go," he added. "Stay out of it. You've done enough." He hung up the phone.

"Harsh," Luke murmured as they hiked quickly back to Rick's Expedition.

"She wants to go after Cordero and his men. Probably without backup, since that seems to be her way." J.D. pulled out his SIG and checked the clip. Full. One in the chamber. And three boxes of ammo stored in his lightweight backpack in the Expedition. "But I need her to stay safe."

Rick followed his directions to Route 8. At the crossroads, his cousin looked at J.D. "We should split up. Surround them."

J.D. nodded. "Jake, you and Gabe take the north entrance. It'll be the most exposed, and you're the best trackers. Luke and Sam, circle around from the west. Rick and I'll come from the southeast. Keep your phones on vibrate and text as needed."

"Wish I had a radio," Rick grumbled as he handed the keys to Luke, who they agreed would park the SUV on the western edge of the woods before they hiked in. He and J.D. set off on foot toward the south, looking for a likely entrance spot to the dense piney woods. They reached a break in the underbrush growing like weeds along the edge of the roadside. "Quiet from here on," J.D. warned. Rick answered with a nod.

They entered the woods, heading northwest.

MIKE WAS SO SCARED HE could barely think straight, but so far he hadn't cried once. He considered that a victory.

Cordero's men hadn't hidden their conversation from him, rattling off their plans in Spanish. He guessed they thought he didn't know how to speak the language. He didn't let them know he did.

His dad had taught him and Cissy both to speak the language when he was little, and then his Aunt Abby had taken his Spanish lessons to a whole new level when she moved to Gossamer Ridge last winter. She said he was a natural. He guessed he was, because even though the men holding him captive spoke rapid-fire Spanish with a thick accent, he was able to keep up with most of it.

They were using him to get to his Uncle Luke. After they had Luke, they'd kill everyone else they could get their hands on.

Mike couldn't let that happen. He knew his dad thought he hadn't been a good father to him and Cissy, but he was wrong. His dad had taught him the really important lessons. Like doing the right thing, no matter the cost. Taking care of your family, no matter what.

He had no doubt his father was already on the way to find him. Sooner or later, he'd show up. And he'd be killed on sight.

So Mike had to get away from the thug holding him captive before that happened.

He wasn't sure where the rest of the men were—maybe in that crumbling building about a half mile through the woods. They seemed to be using it as a base of operations. But for some reason, they put Mike and his prison guard in a small tent deeper in the woods, away from Cordero and his men.

The thug's name was Manuel. He looked slow-witted and sleepy. Mike guessed they'd stuck poor Manuel with Mike because they didn't consider a thirteen-year-old kid any sort of threat, especially if he was bound hand and foot.

Another mistake.

Manuel's eyes drifted shut. A second later, he left out a snuffling snore. Mike waited to see if the sound would wake him.

It didn't. Mike quickly bent and pulled his legs through his arms, bringing his bound hands to the front of the body. From there, he twisted until he could reach his right pocket, where he kept his pocket knife. Idiots hadn't even searched him for weapons. Apparently they didn't have a high opinion of the resourcefulness of American youth.

He'd like to introduce them to his Boy Scout troop.

He pulled out the knife from the pocket and flicked it open, keeping his eyes on Manuel. The guard kept snoring lightly.

With a few strokes of the sharp blade, Mike made quick work of the plastic cuffs binding his hands. He cut the cuffs on his feet and stretched his limbs, wincing as they painfully tingled back to life. Manuel sat between him and the tent exit, but his knife would make quick work of the thin nylon. He just had to find a way to cut through without making a lot of noise.

He could slip out beneath the tent if he could just open about fifteen inches with his knife. It would be enough to allow him to shimmy under the nylon.

Keeping one eye on Manuel, Mike sliced through the nylon, doing his best to muffle the sound with his body. He slit open about twelve inches without waking Manuel and decided it would be enough. Listening hard, he tried to hear if they had put any guards outside the tent. He heard nothing—no coughs, no breathing, no footsteps on the loamy forest floor.

Now or never, he thought.

In one swift movement, he slid under the tear in the tent and escaped into the woods. Outside, he paused, waiting to hear Manuel rumble to life inside. But all he heard was another soft snuffling sound.

He let himself breathe before the black spots forming

behind his eyes started moving together into a void. Warm, humid air rushed into his lungs, breathing hope into him.

The warehouse and Eladio Cordero's men lay north.

Mike headed south.

THERE WAS AN OLD DIRT track that led through Hansbury Woods from the south. Nobody used it anymore, now that the Gray Trading Company had become Gray Global Partners, moving their warehouse and distribution center to the port city of Mobile. But the faint footprint of the old access road remained to guide Natalie quickly north toward the warehouse.

They would have a perimeter set up. Something to warn them of intruders. She'd studied *El Cambio* and the cartels a bit when she was preparing for a Homeland Security drill. So she knew they believed strongly in eschewing high-tech security. They believed it created more problems than it solved—especially for the largely poor and uneducated street thugs who made up the bulk of their merry little band of killers and torturers. So she kept an eye out for human scouts, who'd probably make up the first line of defense against intruders.

She saw movement in her peripheral vision and froze, turning her head slowly. Someone was coming through the woods at a quick but furtive pace.

She could see only movement at first, a swish of a bush, the shimmy of a tree as someone passed close by. But after a few seconds, the person came into view for a brief moment. Her breath caught, hot and tight in her chest.

Mike.

She started moving toward him, only to see him reverse course, moving in a zigzag to the southwest. She didn't dare call out to halt his forward movement, but she was afraid that his sudden rush would send him headlong into a perimeter guard.

She ran to catch up, not bothering with stealth. She saw

him turn his head for a second to see who was in pursuit. His eyes widened almost comically when he spotted her.

He stopped in place and let her catch up, throwing himself into her arms as soon as she was close enough.

She hugged him close, stroking his sweat-dampened hair. "Shh. I've got you."

"They're in a warehouse—they were keeping me in a tent, but the guard fell asleep—we have to get out of here!" He spoke in a rattling whisper, his eyes lifting to meet hers. "Now."

She nodded, heading him south again. But they hadn't gone twenty yards when a volley of shots rang out behind them, splintering a nearby tree. Natalie pushed Mike firmly in front of her and kept going, turning only long enough to return fire.

"There'll be a dozen guys on us in seconds," Mike gasped as he ran wildly in front of her.

She knew he was right. But there was no alternative to running. And as long as she kept herself—and the rifle plates in her Kevlar vest—between the shooter and Mike, he had a chance to escape.

"Just run," she called to him, picking up speed.

GUNFIRE SPLIT THE AIR, a rat-a-tat volley that J.D. knew came from an AK-47. It came from surprisingly close by—no more than a couple of hundred yards.

Beside him, Rick spat out an answering round of profanities. J.D.'s pocket vibrated. He almost ignored it until he realized his brothers might know more about the gunfire than he did.

But it was Gabe, asking if he knew where the gunfire had come from. Close by, J.D. answered and sent the text.

"Someone's coming," Rick whispered.

A second later, J.D. heard crashing sounds in the woods nearby, and spotted a flash of blue streaking through the trees. Mike—that was his blue T-shirt, he realized, his heart rattling like a snare drum.

Without another thought, he dashed forward into the woods, uncaring whether or not his son's pursuers spotted him. Running at an angle, he raced to intercept Mike before the unthinkable happened. As he ran, it sank in that his son was not alone.

Natalie was right behind him, her eyes wide with fear but her jaw set with the fierce determination of a mother bear protecting her young. She locked eyes with him for a brief, electric moment, stumbling a little as she hit a ragged patch of undergrowth.

A second later, J.D. spotted the gunman. He was only fifty yards behind them, his rifle aimed squarely at Natalie's back.

J.D. whipped his SIG from the holster and fired, but a split second too late. By the time J.D.'s shot hit him square in the chest, the gunman had already fired two rapid shots toward Natalie and Mike. Natalie made a loud grunting noise and fell facedown in the underbrush.

J.D. scrambled to Natalie's side, his heart filling his throat. *Please God, please God, please God—*

She groaned when he touched her, and he felt the thick shape of a vest under her blouse. Had it done its job?

"I'm okay. I'll never breathe again, but I'm okay," she murmured. "There'll be more coming."

A flurry of gunfire in the distance seemed to punctuate her words. J.D. looked at Rick, torn.

"Get them out of here. I'll go help your brothers." Rick headed into the woods. On the way, J.D. saw, he grabbed the AK-47 from the hands of the dead gunman.

"Can you walk?" J.D. asked Natalie.

She sat up, wincing. "The rifle plate stopped the shot. But man, it hurts."

J.D. helped her up, taking a quick second to look his son

up and down. Mike gazed up at him, his eyes bright with excitement and fear. "You okay, buddy?"

He nodded. "Let's get her to a hospital."

J.D. smiled at his son's solemn words. Kid was growing up right before his eyes.

He called the sheriff's department and found out that units were already on the way to the area. J.D. told them to make sure they had heavy weaponry—they were up against big guns.

They heard the sirens before they reached Route 8. "Is Uncle Luke gonna be okay?" Mike asked as they tried to flag down one of the cruisers zooming up the road.

"I wouldn't want to be those bad guys," J.D. said with a confident smile, though beneath the smile he pasted on for his son's sake, he was terrified that his family was being slaughtered in the woods as they spoke.

"I'm fine," Natalie said. "If you need to go—"

He turned to look at her. Her face was pale and pinched with pain, but her eyes met his with strength and understanding.

"No. I need to be with my son." He lowered his voice. "I need to be with you."

Her eyes melted, but one of the siren-blazing cars slowed to a stop beside them, keeping her from replying. It was Massey in a big black sedan.

"Get in."

"She needs to go to a hospital," J.D. said quickly. "She took a bullet in the vest."

"I'm fine—"

"You're on the way to the hospital," Massey said firmly.

J.D. helped her into the back of the car, trying not to look back at the woods where his family was carrying out the fight of their lives.

I'm where I have to be, he thought.

And knew it was true.

No BROKEN RIBS. No INTERNAL injuries. Just a massive bruise that would hurt for a few days but would do no lasting harm.

Natalie insisted on leaving the E.R. as soon as they gave her a clean bill of health, even though the doctors thought she should rest there overnight, just to be sure. She found J.D. and Mike huddled together in the E.R. waiting room, their eyes on Massey, who stood outside on the terrace, talking on the phone.

"Any news?" she asked.

J.D. whipped his head around. "The shooting's over. We're waiting to hear the casualty count." He cocked his head. "Should you be out of bed?"

She smiled, wishing Mike weren't in earshot. "Just a bruise. I'm fine. Why don't we go to the scene and see what we can find?"

"No need—everyone at the scene is headed here." Massey had come back inside now and crossed to where they sat. "Nobody's giving me names, Cooper. Sorry. But the survivors should be here any minute."

J.D.'s cell phone rang. He checked the display. "Luke," he said with a soft sigh. He headed outside to the terrace. Natalie and Mike followed him.

"Luke?" J.D. listened for a second, his eyes fluttering shut. A smile crept over his face, and Natalie felt a weight lift from her chest. Opening his eyes again, he saw their interested looks and punched the speaker button.

"Cordero's dead. I killed him myself," Luke said. "We're all fine—Jake twisted his ankle, but it should be fine by morning. Cordero and his crew didn't seem to think we'd try an ambush of our own. Hell, maybe they bought their own hype."

"Where are you now?" J.D. asked.

"In Rick's Expedition. We're on our way to the hospital."

"See you when you get here."

They went back into the waiting room. "All the Coopers accounted for," J.D. told Massey with a grin.

"I wasn't betting against y'all," Massey replied. He looked at Mike. "You hungry, Mike? I saw a vending machine down the hall. My treat."

Mike looked at his father, as if for permission. J.D. nodded, and Mike headed off with Massey.

J.D. turned to Natalie. "I think Massey wanted to give us some alone time."

She looked up at him, trying to read his mind. She hadn't really bought his dismissive tone on their last phone call—she knew he'd been trying to protect her from Cordero and his men. But did that really change anything? He was still a man who'd held a torch for his dead wife for over a decade. Solving her murder might not change anything.

"I don't want to say goodbye to you," he said bluntly.

Or, maybe, she thought, solving Brenda's murder had changed everything. "So don't."

"I have to go back to Gossamer Ridge. My whole family's there. My brother's getting married and my parents depend on me to keep things running at the Marina. And Mike's starting high school this fall and he's really looking forward to it—"

"I'm not asking you to give up your life," she said softly.

"Are you asking anything at all?"

It was an excellent question, she realized. What did she really want from J.D.? A house, a two-car garage, two kids and a collie in the fenced-in backyard?

"I want you to want to be with me more than you want anything else in the world," she blurted aloud, realizing with immediate mortification what a huge commitment she'd just asked him to make.

"Okay," he answered. "Anything else?"

She stared at him. "That's it? No negotiation?"

His mouth curved in slow, sexy grin. "You don't negotiate

with someone who's giving you everything you want, sugar." He bent and kissed her, a slow, sweet kiss that deepened so gradually that she was halfway to unconsciousness before she realized just what a spectacle they were making of themselves in the middle of the Ridley County Hospital waiting room.

She tugged until he let her go, but only far enough to wrap his arms around her waist. She traced the broad contour of his chest through his T-shirt. "I've been thinking about leaving Terrebonne for a while. Even before Carric's murder. Guess this is as good an excuse as I'll ever get."

"How soon can you move?"

She laughed. "I don't know. There are things to take care of." Her laughter faded. "Soon. I promise."

He stroked her hair. "This Saturday?"

"For a visit or for good?" she asked.

"Your choice." He dropped a kiss on her temple and whispered in her ear. "Either way, you have a bouquet to catch."

Epilogue

Brenda's grave was sheltered by the boughs of an old oak that grew near the edge of Piney Grove Cemetery. J.D. knelt by the granite marker and brushed the leaves away from the base, then ran his fingers across the etched letters of Brenda's name.

"We got him, baby. He's in jail and he's not getting out."

He dropped his hand away from the silent stone, feeling strangely alone. So many times, when he'd visited this place, he'd felt Brenda's presence like a warm breath against his cheek; but all he felt now was a light summer breeze drifting over him.

She was gone. She'd been gone for years, in a better place than this screwed-up world he still lived in. Only his thirst for vengeance had kept her alive for J.D.

But he'd found justice for her. It was done.

He could finally let her go.

"We thought we'd find you here."

J.D. turned to find his daughter, Cissy, standing a few feet away, her arm around her brother's, Mike's, shoulders. He smiled at his children, his chest aching from a bittersweet concoction of love and regret. "Just came by to tell her it's over."

"Is it?" Cissy crossed to him, putting her arm around his waist. "Really over? For you, I mean."

He hugged her tightly. "Yeah."

"And you're ready to move on?"

J.D. glanced at Mike, who was wincing a little at his sister's question. J.D. had told his daughter about Natalie, knowing if he didn't, Mike would beat him to it. He hadn't been sure how his daughter would take the idea of a new woman in his life, but he should have known better. Cissy was thrilled for him and eager to meet Natalie.

"I'm ready," he said aloud, smiling at his daughter.

She gave him a quick squeeze, and even Mike managed a smile. J.D. knew his son liked Natalie a lot more than he liked the idea of his father having a romantic relationship. He'd get over it.

Eventually.

Cissy looked at her watch. "We'd better get a move on. It's almost two."

J.D. gave a start. He hadn't realized it was getting so late. Natalie should be arriving any time now, and he needed to get to the lake house to meet her.

He put his arms around both his children, drawing them with him as they left the cemetery behind. "Come on. We have a wedding to attend."

IT MIGHT BE AARON'S wedding day, but the groom wasn't the only Cooper brother as jumpy as a rabbit. J.D. hadn't heard from Natalie since she'd called as she was leaving Terrebonne for the long drive north that morning. Even with Cordero out of the way, Hamilton Gray and Travis Rayburn remained threats. Catching Gray had closed the door on Brenda's murder, but it hadn't ended the danger. For now Gray was tucked away in the Ridley County Jail, but he was a wealthy man with a long reach who now hated Natalie with all the obsession he'd felt for Brenda.

"Relax," his brother Luke murmured, clapping his shoulder. "She'll be here soon. If she's anything like you've described her, she can handle whatever Gray can throw her way at this point."

Yes, Natalie was tough and capable, but J.D. couldn't be sure just how much power and influence Gray still might be able to wield from jail.

Before he could answer Luke, the door to the study opened, and Gabe burst in, his pretty brunette girlfriend, Alicia, in tow. Alicia held out her left hand, flashing a bright diamond on the ring finger. Her smile was even brighter. "She said yes!" Gabe exclaimed.

Luke hugged Gabe, while J.D. kissed Alicia's cheek. "Run while you can," he murmured in her ear.

"Hey!" Gabe smacked J.D.'s arm. "Don't scare her away."

"J.D., after the wedding, can I pick your brain about Hamilton Gray?" Alicia asked.

Gabe tugged her toward the door. "No shop talk today, Dr. Solano."

"Soon to be Dr. Cooper," Luke added.

"He might become Mr. Solano," Alicia said tartly.

Over her head, Gabe shook his head. *No, I won't,* he mouthed. They left at a sprint, the study door rocking back against the wall as they brushed past.

J.D. laughed. "I don't know which one of them is going to be harder to keep up with."

"Good thing they've got each other." Luke grabbed the tie out of J.D.'s hand. "Here, let me do this for you."

"I think that's my job."

The sound of Natalie's voice in the open doorway made J.D.'s heart skip a beat. She looked like a vision, making him blink a couple of times to make sure he hadn't conjured her up out of sheer desperation to see her.

She was dressed in something green and frothy that seemed to dance over her slender curves, vibrant and alive. Her smile lit up the room like sunshine, and J.D. wanted to bathe in her glow for the rest of his life. "You made it."

She crossed to him, holding her hands out. "I made it."

He clasped her hands in his, then pulled her into a tight hug. "I started to worry when I didn't hear from you."

"I was on the phone with my father most of the drive. He's very involved in making sure none of Cordero's remaining thugs give Bayside Oil any trouble." She lifted her face for a kiss.

He obliged her with fierce hunger, breaking away only when his brother's loud throat-clearing filtered through his brain. He shot his brother a sheepish grin.

Natalie smiled at Luke as she started to tie J.D.'s tie. "Good to see you again, Luke."

"There's a whole heap of Coopers you haven't met yet," Luke warned her. "Including Cissy. I saw her outside, and she was a nervous wreck about meeting her daddy's new squeeze."

Natalie chuckled. "I'm a nervous wreck about meeting her."

"Don't be." J.D. wrapped his arm around her waist. "She already loves you for saving Mike's life."

"We all do," Luke added, his expression going serious.

"He saved me first." Natalie's arm tightened around J.D.'s waist. "He's a brave kid. Crazy, but brave."

Abby, Luke's pretty brunette wife, stuck her head in the door. "Wedding's ready to start, y'all."

J.D. twined his fingers with Natalie's as they followed Luke and Abby to the backyard, where the flattest part now contained rows of chairs for the wedding guests. Aaron and Melissa had opted for a small wedding—mostly family, though Melissa's parents and a few people from Melissa's law firm attended, and a few of Aaron's fellow deputies had managed to align their day off with the wedding.

Aaron's fellow deputy, and brother-in-law, Riley Patterson, was the best man; and Melissa had chosen their sister-in-law—and Riley's wife—Hannah as matron of honor, but that was the extent of the wedding party.

"I thought you said most of the guests would be Coopers," Natalie whispered as she and J.D. settled in their seats behind his father and mother. "This would be a lot of Coopers."

J.D. grinned. "Well, my Uncle Roy and his wife, Jean, have six kids themselves. You met Rick in Terrebonne." He pointed out Rick's dark head in the crowd. "That's his eldest brother, Jesse, over there by the hydrangea—" J.D. craned his neck to find the rest of his cousins, but processional music started playing on the stereo system on his parents' deck above, forcing him to pay attention to the wedding.

It was the first time he was able to sit through one of his siblings' weddings without aching with regret for Brenda's loss: he realized with surprise after the smiling bride and groom kissed to seal their union. In line to congratulate the happy couple, he turned and caught Natalie's hand in his. She gazed up at him with a sexy spark of heat she seemed to throw off every time he touched her.

"Alicia said yes to Gabe today," he told her.

Natalie smiled. "I'll be sure to congratulate them, too."

"They'll be marrying soon—and you know what that means."

She shook her head. "What?"

"I'll be the only single Cooper." He shook his head. "Not a distinction I'm going to like very much."

Her lips curved. "No?"

"No." He kissed her knuckles, grinning as her eyes darkened. "I'll be looking for a wife. Know any prospects?"

Her smile broadened to a grin. "I just might."

Behind him, his brother Jake muttered, "Get a room."

Laughing, J.D. and Natalie moved forward together, hand in hand.

* * * * *

Harlequin

INTRIGUE

COMING NEXT MONTH

Available July 12, 2011

#1287 BY ORDER OF THE PRINCE
Cowboys Royale
Carla Cassidy

#1288 RUSTLED
Whitehorse, Montana: Chisholm Cattle Company
B.J. Daniels

#1289 COWBOY FEVER
Sons of Troy Ledger
Joanna Wayne

#1290 HER STOLEN SON
Guardian Angel Investigations: Lost and Found
Rita Herron

#1291 BAYOU BODYGUARD
Jana DeLeon

#1292 DEAL BREAKER
The McKenna Legacy
Patricia Rosemoor

> You can find more information on upcoming
> Harlequin® titles, free excerpts and more at
> **www.HarlequinInsideRomance.com.**

HICNM0611

REQUEST YOUR FREE BOOKS!
2 FREE NOVELS PLUS 2 FREE GIFTS!

◊ Harlequin®

INTRIGUE®

BREATHTAKING ROMANTIC SUSPENSE

USA TODAY *bestselling author B.J. Daniels
takes you on a trip to Whitehorse, Montana,
and the Chisholm Cattle Company.*

RUSTLED

Available July 2011 from Harlequin Intrigue.

As the dust settled, Dawson got his first good look at the
rustler. A pair of big Montana sky-blue eyes glared up at
him from a face framed by blond curls.

A woman rustler?

"You have to let me go," she hollered as the roar of the
stampeding cattle died off in the distance.

"So you can finish stealing my cattle? I don't think so."
Dawson jerked the woman to her feet.

She reached for the gun strapped to her hip hidden under
her long barn jacket.

He grabbed the weapon before she could, his eyes nar-
rowing as he assessed her. "How many others are there?"
he demanded, grabbing a fistful of her jacket. "I think you'd
better start talking before I tear into you."

She tried to fight him off, but he was on to her tricks and
pinned her to the ground. He was suddenly aware of the soft
curves beneath the jean jacket she wore under her coat.

"You have to listen to me." She ground out the words
from between her gritted teeth. "You have to let me go. If
you don't they will come back for me and they will kill
you. There are too many of them for you to fight off alone.
You won't stand a chance and I don't want your blood on
my hands."

"I'm touched by your concern for me. Especially after
you just tried to pull a gun on me."

"I wasn't going to shoot you."

Dawson hauled her to her feet and walked her the rest of the way to his horse. Reaching into his saddlebag, he pulled out a length of rope.

"You can't tie me up."

He pulled her hands behind her back and began to tie her wrists together.

"If you let me go, I can keep them from coming back," she said. "You have my word." She let out an unladylike curse. "I'm just trying to save your sorry neck."

"And I'm just going after my cattle."

"Don't you mean your boss's cattle?"

"Those cattle are mine."

"*You're* a Chisholm?"

"Dawson Chisholm. And you are…?"

"Everyone calls me Jinx."

He chuckled. "I can see why."

Bronco busting, falling in love…it's all in a day's work.
Look for the rest of their story in

RUSTLED

Available July 2011 from Harlequin Intrigue
wherever books are sold.

HIEXP0711R

Harlequin®

ROMANTIC
SUSPENSE

Secrets and scandal ignite in a danger-filled,
passion-fuelled new miniseries.

**Family. Lies.
Full exposure.**

When scandal erupts, threatening California Senator
Hank Kelley's career and his life, there's only one place he can
turn—the family ranch in Maple Cove, Montana. But he'll need
the help of his estranged sons and their friends to pull the family
together despite attempts on his life and pressure from a sinister
secret society, and to prevent an unthinkable tragedy that would
shake the country to its core.

Collect all 6 heart-racing tales starting July 2011 with
Private Justice
by *USA TODAY* bestselling author
MARIE FERRARELLA

Special Ops Bodyguard by **BETH CORNELISON** (August 2011)
Cowboy Under Siege by **GAIL BARRETT** (September 2011)
Rancher Under Cover by **CARLA CASSIDY** (October 2011)
Missing Mother-To-Be by **ELLE KENNEDY** (November 2011)
Captain's Call of Duty by **CINDY DEES** (December 2011)

Harlequin

SPECIAL EDITION

Life, Love and Family

THE TEXANS ARE COMING!

Reader-favorite miniseries Montana Mavericks
is back in Special Edition with new loves,
adventures and more.

July 2011 features *USA TODAY* bestselling author
CHRISTINE RIMMER
with
RESISTING MR. TALL, DARK & TEXAN.

A Texas oil mogul arrives in Thunder Canyon on
business and soon falls for his personal assistant. Only
one problem—she's just resigned to open a bakery!
Can he convince her to stay on—as his bride?

Find out in July!

Look for a new
Montana Mavericks: The Texans Are Coming **title**
in each of these months

August	September	October
November	December	

Available wherever books are sold.

www.Harlequin.com

SEMM0711

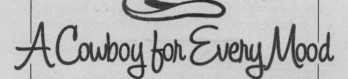

UNRAVEL THE MYSTERY

FIGURE COUNTING:

How many triangles are there
in the diagram?

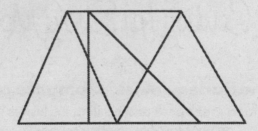

**FIND YOUR ANSWERS in next month's
INTRIGUE titles, available July 12!**